The
Empty House
Mystery

THE EMPTY HOUSE
MYSTERY

By Norvin Pallas

ACKNOWLEDGMENTS

The Wildside Press reprints of the Ted Wilford series were made possible by the assistance of many people, including Norvin Pallas's family; Steve Romberger, whose copy of *The Secret of Thunder Mountain* was ultimately used to create this edition; George Beatty and James D. Keeline, who provided copies of many of the texts and covers; and David M. Baumann, whose essay "A Dark Horse Series" was an invaluable reference for reprinting the stories; and of course Wildside's production team, Shawn Garrett, Helen McGee, and Sam Hogan.

Published by Wildside Press LLC.
www.wildsidepress.com

To Janet

Contents

1.

An Alley Chase

THE MOVIE ended early, and not waiting for the rerun of the main feature, Ted Wilford and his friend, Nelson Morgan, left the theater and stepped into the brightly lighted lobby. They had gone to the movies alone, but by chance had run into a party of their school friends. Now they were all leaving together, and gathered in a group in the lobby, still blinking a little and talking about the show.

"Wasn't it a wonderful picture?" asked Margaret Lake enthusiastically. "So true to life."

"Not enough excitement," Cliff Corby responded with a little grimace. "Say, it's still early. How about a hamburger and a malted, gang?"

There was a chorus of approvals, but Ted did not join in.

"What's the matter, Ted?" asked Wayne Bell. "You on a diet?"

"No, on an allowance," Cliff kidded him.

"Not exactly," Ted responded to Wayne, giving Cliff only the slightest glance, "but I don't know where I'd put anything more after all that popcorn."

Nelson looked as though he could always eat something more, but he, too, declined.

"Sorry, but we both promised to be home by ten-thirty. Of course I could telephone—"

"Sure you could," Helen Howland urged him. "After all, you only graduate once—from high school, anyway."

"And that's once more than I expected to make it," Nelson joked.

He looked at Ted questioningly. Ted hesitated only a moment. They hadn't wanted to barge in on the party, but now they were convinced they would be fully welcome. This would be their last get-together before graduation.

"Sure, let's go," Ted agreed. "Of course I'll have to call home first—"

"Yes, and I've got to get my car out of the parking lot before it closes," Nelson added. "Why don't you people go on ahead, and we'll be there in a little while?"

He and Ted left the others and turned toward the parking lot. This lot was an enclosure occupying some of the waste space behind the theater and stores. The quickest way to reach it was down a little alleyway alongside the theater, which also served as an emergency fire exit from the theater. It was too narrow for cars. They reached the parking lot by way of a wider alley opening on the other side of the block.

The boys were about to step into the alley when a man approached and motioned to them.

"Say, fellows, have either of you seen a little dog around here?"

"No, we haven't," Nelson returned. "What did he look like?"

It occurred to Ted that as long as they hadn't seen any dog it didn't matter much what he looked like, but he let Nelson take the lead.

"A little white puppy—about five months old—with brown spots around the eyes and on his sides, and a curled-up tail. Named Sandy, but he doesn't answer to that or anything else." Although apparently worried about his dog, the man seemed friendly.

"I guess not," said Nelson regretfully.

"I was parked in front of Larry's Drugstore while I went shopping at the center. I rolled down the window a little to make sure he got enough air. I didn't think he could squirm out, but apparently he did. Either that or someone reached in and opened the door."

"Was he a valuable dog?" Ted questioned.

"No, not a show dog or anything like that, but the children were attached to him. I'd like very much to get him back. A man I met thought he might have seen a dog coming this way. I couldn't find Sandy anywhere on the main street, but I thought he might have turned up this alley. I hesitated about following him because I'm a stranger in town and didn't want people to think I was prowling around in the dark where I didn't belong."

"That's perfectly all right," Ted assured him. "A lot of theater customers use this alley to reach the parking lot. We'll be glad to help you look for your dog if you want us to."

"I'd be awfully grateful if you did. He's very skittish—will probably run if you approach him."

"Why don't we go around the other way?" Nelson suggested. "I've got a flashlight in my car, and that should help. Then we'll come down the alley and you'll come up, and maybe we'll trap him between us."

This plan was agreed upon, and Ted and Nelson walked around the block to reach the parking lot from the other side. After getting Nelson's flashlight from his car, they proceeded back down the alley, flashing the light carefully into all the small nooks and hiding places along the way. In this fashion they made their way ahead slowly.

The stranger was also advancing very slowly, until suddenly, with Nelson's flashlight diverted to the side, he nearly bumped into them.

"Any sign of him?" asked Nelson.

"No, but I noticed another little alley leading off this one and going back of the stores. I didn't see him, but I thought I heard something. I hope I'm not bothering you too much, but—"

"Not at all," Nelson responded. "Might as well see what we can find."

Fifty feet back, the man showed them the alley where he thought he had heard the noise. This was a wider one where deliveries were made to the stores. It was also dotted with numerous rubbish containers and other items of trash that hadn't found their way into containers—presenting a completely different appearance from the bright store fronts on the main avenue. Dutifully Nelson flashed his beam around each container, but without flushing out anything.

"Wait!" the man called. "Over there!"

Nelson followed with the light, but by the time it reached the spot at which the man was pointing, whatever he had seen was gone.

"I thought I saw something moving. It went around that little corner."

They turned into another short, narrow alleyway leading to the rear entrances of two more buildings. It led only about thirty feet, however, before it was crossed and barred with a high wooden fence.

"Look! There he is—crawling through the hole in the fence!"

The boys hadn't yet spotted the dog, but they followed the man's lead to the fence. The opening was too small for them to get through, but having come this far they were unwilling to abandon the chase.

"Over the fence we go," Nelson chanted, beginning to pick up the spirit of the hunt.

"Give me a boost up," Ted ordered, falling in with the

scheme. He went over the fence in a vault, and Nelson, also getting a quick boost from their new acquaintance, followed in short order.

"Sorry it's too high for me," the man called after them, "but I'll go around and try to meet you from the other side."

Ten minutes later Ted and Nelson emerged on the opposite side of the block, having jumped across more fences, but without finding any trace of the missing puppy.

"Funny that the puppy would run that way," Nelson speculated. "Most puppies when they're frightened will crouch down and try to hide."

"I guess there are all kinds of dogs," Ted philosophized, "just like there are all kinds of people."

They half-suspected they might miss connections, but the man was ahead of them, waiting on the sidewalk. He seemed subdued at their lack of success but grateful for their efforts.

"Sorry to have put you to all that trouble," he apologized.

"Oh, we didn't mind," Nelson replied. "I haven't jumped over fences like that since I used to soap windows on Halloween and—"

"How long ago?" asked Ted.

"A *long time* ago, son."

They were now on the brightly lighted main street, approaching Larry's Drugstore where the man's car was parked. In the stronger light he seemed to be studying Ted's face.

"Say, don't I know you? Aren't you Ted Wilford, the editor of the Forestdale High School newspaper?"

"Why, yes," said Ted in surprise, "but I don't remember—"

The man laughed at his discomfiture. "My name's Thomas Gray and I live in Ashton. Last winter our lodge had that dinner reception for Senator Halloway, and we invited all the high-school editors—"

"Of course I remember now. This is my friend, Nelson Morgan. I'm sorry I didn't remember you."

"I couldn't expect that," said Mr. Gray, shaking hands with Nelson. "There were so many of us and so few of you. But I remember you very well. I even recall something being said about your being associated with Mr. Dobson on the *Town Crier*."

"Not associated," Ted corrected. "I'm just the high-school correspondent—or was."

"Mr. Dobson has quite a reputation," Mr. Gray went on. "I understand he's considered the leading small-town newspaper editor in the state. It was even said that he could put this Milford exchange through for us on the new thruway, if he decided to crusade for it. Do you know whether he's made any plans for it?"

Mr. Dobson was well known for the zeal with which he promoted worth-while civic undertakings, but Ted's eyes had narrowed.

"He hasn't said anything to me about it."

"Oh, well, I suppose those editors are often on the inside of things. Maybe he already knows whether or not it's been decided to build the Milford interchange."

He seemed to be waiting for Ted to reply, and Ted answered noncommittally, "If he does, you can be sure he wouldn't say anything, either in print or in person."

They had reached Mr. Gray's car, and he unlocked the door. "Well, I appreciate what you've done for me. You look hot—could I buy you boys a bottle of pop?"

"No, thanks," Nelson answered, "we're on our way to join some friends."

"Then I won't keep you any longer. I'm sorry we didn't find the dog, but I'm not giving up entirely. I'll be back in a couple of days to make inquiries. Well, good night."

They raised their hands as he drove off.

"Still want to join the gang?" asked Nelson.

"Why not? Think we look all right?"

"Not all right, but I don't think we'll get kicked out. Glad I wasn't wearing my graduation suit. Tell you, Ted, why don't you call home for me while I go get the car? We can save some time that way."

Ted went into the drugstore. Larry was not particularly busy just then, and noticed Ted's somewhat rumpled appearance.

"Well, what happened to you?"

"Just chased a dog over some back fences."

"Catch him?"

"No," and Ted explained briefly about their adventure.

"No wonder you couldn't find him in the dark, with all those alleyways. I'm pretty fonds of dogs myself. If you want me to, I'll take a look around for him in the morning."

"I think Mr. Gray would appreciate it if you did."

"Do you know how to reach him?"

"Not exactly, but I know the head of his lodge. He can put me in touch with him."

Ted made his personal calls, then decided it might be just as well if he were to put through a call to Mr. Daniels, the president of the Loyal Harts in Ashton. He was grateful for the hospitality Mr. Daniels had showed him, and glad that he might be able to do something in return for one of the members. But when the call had gone through and he had asked Mr. Daniels to give Larry's number to Mr. Gray, Mr. Daniels replied:

"You must have made a mistake, Ted. There's no one named Thomas Gray in our lodge."

"You're certain of that?"

"Very certain, Ted."

After a few more exchanges Ted hung up, feeling very puzzled. He stopped at the counter to talk with Larry.

"Did you notice that car in front of here, Larry, and see the man I was talking to? How long was he parked there?"

"Just about fifteen minutes or so. I saw him drive up and roll down his window."

"Are you sure about that? He said he'd been shopping at the center."

"If he had, it was an awfully quick trip. Did you check the parking meter? That will tell you how long he was there."

"That's right, it would. Of course he could have come back and dropped in another dime—"

"He didn't, though. I watch those cars in front pretty carefully. I don't like people to park in front and go shopping somewhere else. Nothing I can do about it, though, as long as they drop their dimes in the meter."

If Mr. Gray had arrived only fifteen or twenty minutes ago, he certainly couldn't have gone shopping before he met Ted and Nelson. Mr. Daniels had said that Thomas Gray was not a member of their lodge, so it was doubtful if there was such a person as Mr. Gray. And if there wasn't any Mr. Gray, there probably wasn't any dog, either. Larry hadn't mentioned seeing him in the car, and neither Ted nor Nelson had caught a glimpse of him.

When Ted rejoined Nelson, he explained these new developments. Nelson was just as puzzled as he was.

"That was a lot of fun, Ted, but if there wasn't any dog, what were we doing jumping over all those fences, anyway?"

"I wonder," answered Ted with a frown.

2.

Good News and Bad

NOW IT WAS graduation night.

Ted stood in front of the mirror in his room and adjusted his necktie. He was all dressed, except that he would put on his coat later and comb his hair again. Soon his brother Ronald would come chugging up the drive, and then they would have a light supper—just sandwiches and a salad, his mother had said, appreciating that he might be feeling excited and in no mood for a heavy meal. Anyway, there would be plenty to eat later, after the ceremony, when relatives and friends were to meet at his house for a midnight party.

This was the big night, the night he had looked forward to for so many years, seemingly so far away that he secretly doubted it would ever come. He was glad it had arrived at last, but now that it was here it seemed like the end of—so many things. This reverie was broken by the sound of a car on the drive. He ran downstairs and outside, momentarily forgetting his carefully cultivated dignity as a senior.

"Well, how's the graduate?" Ronald greeted him, extending his hand. "Hi, Mom," he added as his mother appeared, and he gave her a kiss. "Everything ready for the big night?"

"All ready, Ronald. We can eat as soon as you're ready." His mother looked at him a little anxiously, not quite certain

11

he was eating properly while living away from home. What she saw evidently reassured her, for she smiled.

"I'd like to have a shower first, if there's time. I feel dusty from that long drive. What's the schedule for tonight? Do I drive you to school, Ted?"

"No, Nelson's picking me up early. But you're to stop at the bus depot for Aunt Alice and Uncle Tracy and the kids. The others are driving in."

Ronald would have been a less-than-astute brother had he not noticed Ted's somewhat depressed air, and he clapped him on the shoulder as they were going upstairs.

"Cheer up, Ted. This isn't the end of everything. Tonight you're looking backward, but tomorrow you'll be looking forward to all the new friends you're going to make and all the possibilities for making a new life for yourself."

Ted reflected that what Ronald had said was true. If a part of his life seemed to be closing, there was just as exciting a part opening up ahead of him. He smiled.

Several calls came for him, from friends making last-minute plans, and a telegram of congratulations from a relative who was unable to come. Then, as Ronald was dressing, he asked:

"Well, Ted, made any plans for this summer?"

"No, nothing definite," said Ted slowly, sitting down backward on the chair and resting his chin on his arm. "There's no baseball team this summer—too many of the fellows are either working or going out of town. I suppose I'll pick up a job of some sort until college opens."

"At the *Town Crier?* I'm sure Mr. Dobson would take you on if you asked him."

"Yes, I'd thought of that, but you know how it is. Carl Allison seems to resent it every time I so much as stick my nose in the newspaper office. I guess maybe I've written my last story for the *Town Crier*. Now that I'm not the high-school correspondent any more, I won't have very much to take me down there."

"Oh, you'll have to stop in and say hello to Mr. Dobson once in a while," Ronald objected, "after he's been so nice to us."

"Yes, I'll do that, but I'll try to work it in when I know Allison isn't around. Well, that's about all the planning I've done."

Ronald nodded. "That fits in swell with what I had in mind. You've been working hard, and I think you could use a vacation. How'd you like to come to the city and stay with me for a few weeks? Of course I have to work, but there'll be enough time left over to show you a pretty exciting time. Maybe you'd like to come down to the newspaper plant and see how a big city paper operates."

"Sounds great!" Ted agreed.

"That's settled, then. We'll call it my graduation present. How about this graduation—any honors coming your way tonight?"

"No, I don't think so. I won a baseball letter, but that was presented at a dinner last week. And I didn't take any scholarship honors. In fact, I've been putting in so much time on the newspaper that I had to do some cramming for the finals. Oh, heck, maybe I'm just making excuses. Maybe I wouldn't have won anyway."

With a few minutes remaining before supper, Ronald leaned back on the bed, stretching out his long legs.

"Well, Ted, what have you been doing for excitement since last I heard?"

Then Ted explained about Mr. Gray, and how he had asked them to help look for his dog.

"Hm," said Ronald thoughtfully, "sounds very peculiar. What do you make of it, Ted?"

"Well, I think Mr. Gray must have known all along who I was. He isn't a member of the lodge in Ashton, but he must have learned I was at that dinner last winter, and made a few other inquiries about me. Then that night he must have found out I was at the movies."

"How could he have found that out?"

"After I left there was a telephone call for me—a man who said he was representing some small college I never heard of. Mom told him I was at the movies. After that it would be a simple matter to find out what time the picture was over, and then he could meet me on our way to the parking lot. I don't think he had any dog. That was just an excuse to strike up an acquaintance in a casual way."

"Could be, if you can explain why he was so anxious to make your acquaintance. What did you talk about?"

"That's just it, Ron—hardly anything at all, except, very casually toward the end, he asked me if I knew anything about the Milford interchange. I don't, of course."

"I haven't been following this Milford situation very well. What's the story on that?"

"Well, you know they're talking about building a new thruway across the state. The final plans haven't been made public, but there's been a lot of talk about the possibility of an interchange at Milford. The farmers at Milford are mostly against it, because they figure the highway would ruin their farms. But a lot of that land might be commercially valuable, with an interchange so close by. I figure that a person might be able to make a barrel of money, if he knew for sure that the interchange was going to be built."

"What made Mr. Gray think you'd know anything about it?"

"Just that I've been in kind of close touch with Mr. Dobson. Mr. Gray seemed to think that if Mr. Dobson were to lead an editorial crusade in favor of the interchange, maybe he could get it built."

"Mm, Mr. Gray might be right just that far," Ronald agreed. "If Mr. Dobson did take a stand, there are a lot of influential people who would listen to him. But if Mr. Dobson did it, it would be because he thought the interchange was a good thing for *everybody*, not just because it helped a few individuals."

Shortly after supper Nelson stopped in front, and Ted left with him. They had little time for talk, except that Nelson did ask unexpectedly:

"By the way, Ted, do you happen to know of any empty houses for rent?"

"Houses for rent? Where have you been? Haven't you heard about the housing shortage?"

"I know, but I've got an aunt and uncle who live near Milford, and if that new interchange is built they'll have to move. They may even decide to pull out ahead of time, so they're looking around. Sometimes houses for rent are advertised in the *Town Crier*."

"How many? Sometimes one or two, but usually none at all."

"Yes, I know that. The idea was that if an ad came in, you might know about it before other people did—"

"Nothing doing, Nelson, my boy, much as I'd like to help out a friend. Maybe other newspapers operate that way, but not Mr. Dobson's."

They met the rest of the seniors who were gathered in a somewhat nervous group backstage. Presently Miss Trisdale, who was in charge of the school newspaper, came in to congratulate the graduating members of the staff. She immediately found herself besieged with requests for additional copies of the graduation number of the *Statesman*.

"Yes, I believe there are a dozen or so copies left over. Ted, you know where they are. Would you like to go upstairs and get them?"

Ted agreed, and taking the keys from her, went upstairs to the darkened newspaper office. He opened the door and switched on the light. There was the desk where he had presided as editor, there under its cover was the typewriter he had used. He remembered with a sentimental twinge all the fun he had had here. But now it was time to say good-by. He found the copies, switched off the light, and hurried downstairs.

The newspapers were distributed, while other students were busy exchanging snapshots, autographs, and information about future plans. Then at last they were summoned on stage.

Eventually they heard the orchestra tuning up, and then the overture, until the curtain was finally raised. From there on the program proceeded smoothly through the students' speeches, the musical numbers, and the rather long commencement address. Then it was time for the awards. Margaret Lake led the girls in scholarship, and Ted remembered that he had forgotten to congratulate her and would have to do so afterward. His own scholarship record was high, but not high enough to merit mention. Other awards followed for special achievements, until only one remained.

"And now for our final award, the service medal, presented to the student who, in the opinion of his fellow graduates and concurred in by the faculty, has contributed the most in service to the school. I take great pleasure in presenting this medal to the editor of the school newspaper, Ted Wilford!"

Ted sat stunned, hardly having the presence of mind to get to his feet, until he felt a shove at his elbow from the boy beside him. He stood up and made his way to the speakers' table as though groping his way through a fog.

"Thank you, Mr. Brackline," he managed to stammer as the presentation was made. "I don't know what I did to deserve this."

Never before had he found himself the center of so much attention; never before had he heard a thousand people applauding just for him. He felt hot and flushed, and sure he was making a spectacle of himself.

At last it came time to distribute the diplomas, and to the strains of "Pomp and Circumstance" the students filed past the speakers' table to receive their folders. Ted saw some of his young cousins waving at him from the audience, but pretended not to notice. He had already spotted his mother and Ronald, along with the other relatives. Over on the other side of the auditorium was Ken Kutler, the reporter for the North Ridge *News-Record*. Although Ted had not seen Mr. Dobson, he supposed he was somewhere in the audience.

The ceremony drew to its close, the curtain was lowered, and the graduates filed backstage. A huge ring was formed and the diplomas circulated quickly until they found their way into the proper hands. Everything was hurried now, since most of the graduates had friends and relatives waiting, and there was time only for quick congratulations and hurried appointments.

Ted was about to leave when he saw Ronald and Ken come to the door. He wondered what they were doing backstage, since it had been agreed to meet at the car.

"Hi, Ken," he greeted his old friend, and extended his hand. "Glad you could come."

Although Ken shook hands, Ted saw at once that his manner was very preoccupied.

"I'm afraid we have some bad news for you, Ted," Ronald began. "Better tell him, Ken," he decided, as though getting on with an unpleasant duty.

"Ted," said Ken slowly, "I've just had word about Mr. Dobson. He drove his car off the road on his way to the ceremony. He's in the hospital now. It sounds pretty serious."

3.

The Best-Laid Schemes

QUITE SUDDENLY all the pleasure and excitement Ted had felt during the evening vanished, leaving him solemn and depressed. An accident to a valued friend is always a disturbing thing, but this was something more, for Ted had a premonition that the accident might drastically change his own plans for the summer.

"He was driving in from Smithburg," Ken explained, "maybe going a little too fast, as he was trying to get here for the graduation ceremony. Apparently he must have fallen asleep at the wheel. They brought him in to the hospital in Forestdale. I check the police calls the last thing every night, and that's how I just heard of it. I've called the hospital, and they told me they couldn't give me a report on his condition until morning."

"Then I don't suppose it would help any for us to stop out there?" Ronald questioned.

"No, they said specifically no visitors would be allowed."

"He was checking on the farmers' threatened milk strike in Smithburg," Ted reflected. "It must have taken him all day. I suppose he would have stayed there overnight, if it hadn't been for the graduation."

Sensing that Ted was almost trying to blame himself for the accident, Ronald put in practically, "What difference does it make where he was driving? If he hadn't been coming to the graduation, he might have had the accident somewhere else."

"Sure, that's right, Ted," said Ken quickly. "And while I know he wanted to see you graduate, I think he would have covered it as a story, even if you hadn't been in the class."

"What'll we do now?" Ted inquired of his brother. "I don't feel much like going ahead with the party."

"I don't either, but what else can we do? We've got a houseful of guests waiting for us. Besides, there's no use being mournful until we find out how bad it really is. Won't you join us, Ken? We'd be glad to have you."

"No, thanks, I've put in a pretty full day myself. Nice work on the medal, Ted. Pretty to look at, and if worse comes to worst, you can always pawn it for a few bucks."

They laughed, for Ken always tried to appear more cynical than he really was.

The party went better than Ted had expected. There was so much excitement and confusion, along with the gifts and congratulations, that he was able to put his troubles aside for a while. His medal came in for examination, and he was asked what he had done to earn it.

"I don't think I did much of anything," he answered, "except serve as editor of the school paper, and I thought that was fun."

"It can be fun and still be important," an uncle advised him, and Ted decided this might be a piece of philosophy worth remembering.

At last the party broke up, and after helping his mother to clear up the worst of the litter, Ted almost fell into bed, and slept dreamlessly. In spite of his late night, he was up before eight. The sun had risen into an unclouded blue sky, and Ted's melancholy of the night before had disappeared. He found that Ronald had been right—today he was looking forward, wondering what his new way of life had to offer. Ronald came down to breakfast a little later, and they had a long, leisurely meal, with Ronald bringing Ted up to date on the happenings of the last couple of months.

Later they went out to Ronald's car. There was no doubt in their minds where they were going, though they hadn't thought to mention it even to each other. They were going to the hospital, of course.

"But we won't be able to see Mr. Dobson, will we?" asked Ted. "Visiting hours aren't till afternoon."

"I don't know," Ronald returned. "Sometimes in an emergency they will let you in. Anyway, I think it's the best way to find out what the score is. They often aren't too informative over the telephone."

The nurse at the desk told them that Mr. Dobson's condition was serious, but she had no further details, nor did she have authority to admit them.

"Dr. Pearson is the physician in charge, and he'll be in on his morning rounds in a little while. Perhaps you'd care to talk it over with him."

"One thing," said Ronald to Ted as they seated themselves in the lobby, "if Mr. Dobson did have any plans for a crusade on the Milford interchange business, this has put an end to it. He'd have to handle something like that himself."

In ten minutes Dr. Pearson came hurrying in. He would have passed them by with a wave of his hand had not Ronald risen to detain him.

"How is Mr. Dobson doing?" Ronald inquired.

"Mm, not too well. I'll be looking in on him a little later. He has a multiple fracture of his leg and possible internal injuries. It's too early to tell about that with any certainty."

"Then you don't know how soon he'll be back on the paper?"

"I'm not even beginning to think about that yet. All I can

say now is that it will be at least a month, and don't regard that as any sort of promise."

"I know this isn't visiting hour," Ronald proceeded, "but is there any chance of our seeing him now?"

"Well"—the doctor looked thoughtful—"I'm not very pleased with the idea of visitors. However, I realize there's the newspaper to think of, and he may have some arrangements to make. You can go up now if he's awake—but only one of you, and only for five minutes."

While Ronald went up to Mr. Dobson's room, Ted sat down again, almost wishing he had something with which to occupy himself. But nothing was needed, for Ronald was back very soon.

"Five minutes and no more." Ronald laughed. "The nurse put me out right on schedule. Evidently when Dr. Pearson gives an order, it's obeyed to the letter."

"How is he?" asked Ted, as they left the hospital and walked down the long sidewalk to the street.

"Not too good, Ted. His leg is in a cast, so he can hardly move, and he seemed a little groggy from drugs. He was rational enough, though."

"What did he say about the accident?"

"Nothing. I'd guess he doesn't exactly remember how it happened. Anyway, we only had time to talk about two things. He had the nurse give me his notes on the milk strike, and asked that I deliver them to the office."

"And the other thing?"

Ronald smiled. "I guess you know what that was, Ted. It was about you."

"Me? What did I do now?"

"Not what you did, but what you're going to do. He wants you to work on the paper, at least until he's able to get back to the office."

Ted was hardly surprised, having sensed that this was what was coming. He didn't mind too much, for newspaper business was always fascinating to him. On the other hand, there were a few not-so-pleasant aspects about it, too, particularly if Mr. Dobson wasn't there to guide him.

"Well, then, I guess I will," he said slowly.

"Sure, Ted, I knew you would. You could hardly do anything else."

"But that means I won't be going back to the city with you," Ted pointed out.

"I know, Ted. I'd thought of that last night. But you can take a rain check, and maybe we'll be able to make it later in the summer. The best-laid schemes of mice and men do something or other that I can't recall at the moment. In any event I'll be home later for my vacation. Anyway, the whole thing will be a good experience for you."

"Getting along with Carl Allison would be an experience for anybody," said Ted wryly. "When do we deliver those notes, now or after lunch?"

"It's still early for lunch. Do you mind going now? Miss Monroe may be waiting for them."

Knowing that Carl Allison never worked overtime, and so wouldn't be there after noon on a Saturday, Ted would have preferred to wait. But realizing he would have to run into Carl sooner or later, he made no objection. Just the same he was glad to find him absent from the office. If they had to quarrel, at least Ted hoped they could keep it private.

Miss Monroe was in and up to her elbows in work. She looked up as they came in, and her rather tired face broke into a smile.

"Ronald, it's surely nice seeing you again. And Ted, though I didn't get to the graduation, I heard about your medal. I know Mr. Dobson would have been so pleased if—"

"We've just come from Mr. Dobson," Ronald broke in,

taking the papers from his pocket and handing them to her.

"Then you saw him? I called the hospital this morning, but they said visitors weren't allowed."

"I guess we're privileged characters. Oh, by the way, Miss Monroe, in case you haven't heard, let me introduce you to your new assistant."

"Ted? No, I hadn't heard, but I'm very pleased." She motioned toward her desk. "So much work's been piling up, I didn't know if I'd get home before midnight."

"Can't we help you?" Ted put in. "If I'm going to work, I might as well start right now."

"Oh, that doesn't seem very fair, Ted. I know you and Ronald have so little time together. Besides, there's so much here that you wouldn't know how to handle."

Ronald pulled up his chair to the desk. "Then I guess there's only one solution. I'll have to get to work, too. Shall I write up that milk-strike story for you?"

"No, Ronald, there's so much background on it that the notes wouldn't cover that I'll have to do it myself. But you could tackle this pile of mail, if you want to."

Newspapers get so much mail that in a small office it is often a physical impossibility to read it all. Fortunately Ronald had had a good deal of experience along that line, and soon was sorting the mail into three piles: letters that required further attention, information that might be of some value, and—the biggest of the three—a large quantity of material that could be dropped into the wastebasket with no loss to anyone.

Since Miss Monroe would now have to write the graduation story, she had to ask Ted for some of the details. He found that she intended to mention his service medal prominently, and nothing he could say would induce her to change her mind. Then he was put to work at a number of tasks that involved a good deal of trotting back to the printing room in the rear, where Mr. White and his assistant were busy at work. As noon approached, Carl Allison called in, and reported that he wouldn't return to the office that day. Ted felt relieved, although he knew Carl was going to be in for a surprise when Monday rolled around. Still, knowing of Mr. Dobson's accident and how pressed Miss Monroe must be, why hadn't Carl offered to work that Saturday afternoon?

They worked right through the noon hour without stopping to eat. In the room to the rear the two printers had gone home, so that relative quiet had settled over the newspaper office, broken only by the continual jangling of the telephone. But even the telephone calls grew infrequent as one o'clock passed, for very often the office was closed at that hour.

By two o'clock Ronald declared that he didn't see any sense in their working any longer on empty stomachs, and suggested that they take time off for lunch, returning later to finish up. But Miss Monroe wouldn't hear of it, asserting that everything really important had been cleared up and that she wasn't going to impose on them any longer. Both Ted and Ronald had been rather enjoying themselves and had no objection to continuing, but they noticed that Miss Monroe was looking well below par, and didn't want to keep her there any longer than necessary.

Miss Monroe extended her hand to Ronald. "Well, Ronald, I suppose it will be quite a while before you get home again."

"Not too long, I hope. Meanwhile, I could advise you about a good wrestling grip I used to keep Ted in line when he needed it."

"How many years ago?" Ted retorted, and the group broke up with laughter.

Earlier they had telephoned their mother they would be late for lunch, and now they offered to make it for themselves, with Ronald demonstrating the newly acquired skill picked up in his bachelor quarters. Maybe he did better in the city, but here, as smoke began to fill the kitchen, their mother hurried out to the rescue.

That evening Ted and Ronald sat up late talking. Ted was especially interested in the newspaper business just now as he was about to take his place in the field itself, and Ronald was able to supply him with many little tips that Ted thought he might find useful on the job. But on one thing Ronald refused to commit himself—the problem of getting along with Carl Allison.

"That's something you'll have to work out for yourself, Ted. Getting along with your fellow workers is one of the most important requirements for success in the business world, but I admit you do have a special problem."

"I just can't figure him out," Ted pondered. "What's he got to gain by being such a grouch?"

"Don't take it too seriously, Ted. He may be covering up something else that he doesn't want the world to see."

Ronald had just one more piece of advice for Ted, which he saved until the last moment as they headed up the stairs.

"I'm confident you'll be able to handle any problems that come along, Ted. But there's one thing—if you ever get in a real jam, don't hesitate to call on Ken Kutler. He's a right guy."

4.

Lost and Found

EARLY MONDAY morning Ted reported to the office half an hour before it customarily opened. Neither Miss Monroe nor Carl had arrived yet, but he had no trouble getting in, for the printer was already busy at work.

What to do first, Ted wondered. He supposed he ought to fix himself up a place to work. There were only two desks in the office, Miss Monroe's and Mr. Dobson's, and somehow it seemed presumptuous for him to take the editor's desk. Because Carl was out of the office most of the time, he did not have a regular desk, but there was a typing table at which he sat to write up his stories. Ted decided the best thing to do was to use this table, and he pulled it over into position where it would be handier to the light, phone, and files.

He wasn't sure what he ought to do next, although he knew there was plenty to be done. From his own knowledge of newspaper work, and from his experience on Saturday, he knew just about what stage of production the paper had reached. The *Town Crier*, which came out twice a week, on Tuesday and Friday mornings, had two news deadlines: Monday noon and Thursday noon. But even before the deadline most of the paper had already been made up. The type-written stories went to the printer, where they were set up in type and printed on long galley sheets. These galleys went back to the office, were read for errors, and then Miss Monroe cut the stories apart and pasted them on a large sample paper called a dummy. The dummy was now almost complete, except for holes of two kinds: for pictures, or cuts, and late news stories for which space had been reserved.

Although reporters on the trail of hot news hate to admit it, most newspaper stories are the kind that can be anticipated. Should an unexpected big story break at the last moment, the front page has to be broken apart and rearranged. As far as Ted knew, their paper that morning had a space reservation for only one big story. A local boy, Floyd Ambers, who had broken several track records in the Olympics and then gone on an extended tour, was just returning to town. A civic celebration was being planned for him at the railroad station, complete with brass band, speech from the mayor, and parade through town.

Advertising was something Ted knew a good deal less about than he did the news angle, but he was aware that the display advertising—the large blocks—was supposed to be in by Friday night. The classified columns, however, were held open until the last minute, having the same deadline as the news stories.

The telephone rang twice—once a wrong number and once a caller asking for Miss Monroe. Ted explained that she hadn't come in yet, and the caller thanked him and hung up. Except for answering the phone, Ted decided he'd better not try to do anything until Miss Monroe got in and could direct him. Otherwise, he might only add to the confusion with which any newspaper office is already well supplied.

Promptly on time the door opened and Carl came in. He seemed surprised to see Ted there, but Ted was soon convinced that he was only pretending.

"Well, if it isn't the schoolboy wonder editor, come down to show us how a newspaper ought to be run."

"I'm here because Mr. Dobson asked me to help out till he gets back," Ted replied evenly, determined, if there was going to be a quarrel, it would have to be Carl who started it.

"I'll bet that took a lot of coaxing, didn't it? I see you've even made yourself at home at my table and typewriter. I should have thought you'd like to sit in the editor's big swivel chair and act like a real big shot."

"He doesn't have a typewriter on his desk," Ted pointed out mildly.

"So the boy wonder knows how to type," said Carl with unveiled sarcasm. "Maybe he even knows how to do something else that might be useful around here. You'll find a broom over in the closet, and the wastebaskets ought to be emptied."

Ted found his temper rising but controlled himself. Miss Monroe would be in soon, and Carl would be leaving, and after that he could settle down to work.

"I think it's up to Miss Monroe to tell me what to do," Ted retorted. "I'm just waiting till she gets in. She's five minutes late already."

"So she's five minutes late for once in her life. That's a big deal, isn't it? Well, I'm on my way down to the railroad station. Too bad you'll miss the parade, little boy. Tell Miss Monroe I'll phone my story in, and after that I'm going out to Riverhaven. I may not be back to the office all day. Aren't you lucky?"

After Carl had gone, Ted considered what he had said about the wastebaskets. It was true they ought to be emptied, and there was some dusting to be done, and as long as he had a little time to spare he thought he might as well do it. He was determined to show that he wasn't too proud to do some of the small, unpleasant tasks that enter into every job.

By the time he was finished, Miss Monroe still hadn't come in, and Ted was beginning to wonder about it when the telephone rang. This time it was Miss Monroe, and she didn't sound very cheerful.

"Ted, I'm not feeling very well today, and I guess I just won't try to get down to the office. I hate to run out when we're shorthanded already, but I think you'll be able to manage."

"Sure I can," said Ted with more confidence than he felt. "What seems to be the trouble?"

"Oh, a little touch of flu, I guess. My stomach is so upset that I can hardly move. Has Carl come in yet?"

"Yes, he left about ten minutes ago. He's going down to the railroad station, and said he'd phone his story in, and then he's going to Riverhaven."

"All right, Ted, then it's up to you. You'll find the dummy in the middle drawer of my desk. Get it out, will you?"

Ted did, and Miss Monroe continued: "Now everything that's pasted on the dummy is all right. If I were down there, there are a few little things I'd change, but under the circumstances you'd better let it alone. Those stories have been proofread, and the cuts are O.K. Now the first column on the front page is the space I saved for the Olympics story. You'll be able to write that up when Carl phones, and put a Number Ten headline over it—you'll find the requirements in the style book. The other open places on the dummy are for stories which were handed to the printer on Saturday, and the galleys haven't come in yet. He'll have them ready for you soon. Those stories will have to be carefully read for errors. Then you can paste them on the dummy, in the spaces I've marked. I don't think any of them will be too short, but if they're too long you'll have to cut a little off the ends. All right?"

"Yes, I guess I've got all that," Ted agreed.

"All right, then, Ted, thanks," but her voice sounded a little dissatisfied. Ted supposed that she would have liked to give him some further instructions but was afraid she would only confuse him.

"Good-by, Miss Monroe. Take care of yourself," he said, and they hung up.

Jack, the printer's assistant, came in a little later with the galleys, and Ted went to work reading them carefully. He quickly found and corrected all the printing errors he could locate. He also checked all local names and addresses, but out-of-towners could not be checked very readily, except to compare the proof with the original stories. As to the facts, he had to assume they were accurate, unless a person or organization was spoken of in an unfavorable manner, when he knew special care must be exercised to avoid any possibility of libel. Fortunately, except for a couple of traffic arrests, nothing like that came up. Ted returned the galleys to the printing room for correction, and when the galleys came back to him, he cut them up and mounted them on the dummy.

Headlines were another problem. Until she began to assemble the dummy, Miss Monroe did not know just where a story would be placed and what kind of headline it would require. For this reason headlines were on a separate galley. Most of the headlines had already been cut out and pasted on the dummy. In other places they were merely written in with pencil, and Ted cut out the missing headlines from the galley and mounted them. The paper was now fairly complete, except for Carl's story. The parade had evidently taken place as scheduled, for Ted could hear the music of the band, although the procession had not come down their street.

Carl phoned a little later, asking for Miss Monroe, and when he learned she was ill he almost exploded.

"Holy mackerel!"

"You'd better give me the story so I can write it up," Ted replied steadily but with little enthusiasm.

"You got rocks in your head or something? You think I'd

let you mutilate my story for me? I can't stop in at the office or I'll miss my appointment in Riverhaven, but get your typewriter ready and give me a few moments to get it organized and I'll dictate it to you,"

In the movies a reporter often dictates a story over the phone, but in real life he generally phones in the facts, and the story is written in the office. But this time, because of Carl's distrust of Ted's ability, they would do it in movie fashion. Ted moved over to Miss Monroe's desk and put a sheet of paper in the typewriter. She had a clip on her phone to fasten it to her head, leaving her hands free, and Ted put it on.

"All ready," he announced.

Slowly and with frequent pauses Carl dictated his story. Because Carl had to stop to think, Ted was able to type just about as fast as Carl could talk, and it pleased him that he didn't have to ask Carl to wait.

"All right, wrap it up," Carl said as he finished, and hung up.

Ted read the story over and corrected a couple of typing errors he found. Then he got out the style book and in a short while was able to compose a headline that had the necessary number of letters on each line. He took the story back to the printing room.

Now that he had a little time to think, Ted began to wonder about Miss Monroe. Surely she would have come to the office this morning—their deadline morning—if she could possibly have made it. He knew that Miss Monroe lived alone in a small apartment. He didn't feel he should call and possibly bother her to no purpose. However, it occurred to him that he could call his mother and see how she felt about it. He dialed his home number.

When his mother answered, Ted explained about Miss Monroe's illness.

"I was just wondering, Mom, what you'd think about

stopping over there and seeing her. She doesn't have any-body with her, you know."

"Yes, Ted, maybe that would be a good idea. I'll be shop-ping in that neighborhood, and can make it look as though I'd just dropped in."

"And you'll call me and let me know?"

"Yes, Ted, just as soon as I find out anything. How are you making out?"

"Fine," Ted replied with a little glow of pride which was probably unmerited, for he had gotten along so well mostly because Miss Monroe had left everything in such good shape.

The proof on the Olympics story came back and Ted checked it and returned the entire dummy. That seemed to be that. He wondered when Miss Monroe would be back, and what plans he ought to be making for the next issue. And suddenly that little glow left him, for the thought of getting out the paper without Miss Monroe's help was more than a little frightening. He began to think of all the things he didn't know how to handle, and wondered what he would do if that nightmare happened to come true.

The telephone rang again.

"The *Town Crier* office," Ted announced.

"Ah—I'd like to place an ad in your lost-and-found column. Is it too late to make your edition for tomorrow morning?"

Ted had fondly hoped that he was all through with this issue, but he knew that advertising is a newspaper's life blood, and while only a small sum is involved in each in-dividual case, it is necessary to keep the channels open and ready to serve the public.

"I guess we can still take it," he decided, drawing a pad and pencil toward him. He could visualize the classified column. There was no room now for an extra ad, but he could cut the last line of the news story above and move the whole thing up. "What did you lose?"

"Well, it's a notebook, a dark red leather notebook with a zipper running around the edge—you know the kind I mean. You don't have to put all that in—just say a notebook in a green folding envelope. Whoever found it will know what it means. I lost it this morning either on the train between Stanton and Forestdale, or else in the station at Forestdale—there was so much confusion there this morning, brass band and everything. This isn't Flag Day, is it?"

"No, just a welcoming celebration for a hero. Are you going to offer a reward? That sometimes helps a little."

"Reward? Well, I don't mind paying a reward, although it's hard to put a value on something like this. It contains personal papers that wouldn't be worth anything to anyone else, but if I don't get them back I'm just about dead." He laughed ruefully. "Yes, say 'reward,' but don't put down any amount."

"All right—and your phone number?"

"My phone number is—oh, could you put this in with a box number? I know that's a little unusual, but I'm going to be away from home so much that a person trying to call me might get discouraged and give up."

"Well, O.K., if that's the way you want it," said Ted, a little dubiously. "How many insertions did you want?"

"Oh, I guess one will be enough. The person who found it will be looking for an ad, I suppose. If he doesn't see it—or doesn't want to see it—I guess I'm just out of luck."

"Sometimes people who find things turn them over to the police," Ted reminded him.

"That's so, they do, but on a railroad train it's hard to know just which police department they might turn it in to. And I'll check with the railroad lost and found, too. Is that all?"

"I guess so. Your name, please?"

"My name's Mr. Denning—Harold Denning, and my telephone number is Forestdale 8106." He laughed again. "I suppose you're wondering about payment."

"You could send a check. I'll look up the advertising rates and tell you how much it will be."

"Oh, don't bother. I think it would be just as easy for me to stop in tomorrow and pay for it in person—and, incidentally, see if you've gotten any answers yet."

"There won't be any answers by tomorrow if you have to wait for a letter."

"I suppose not, but I'll be in anyway. Maybe somebody will telephone in to the office. Well, thanks for your help. Good-by."

Ted wrote out the ad on a special paper provided for that purpose. Mr. Denning had said not to mention that the notebook was of dark red leather with a zipper, but when Ted came to count the lines he found he had three quarters of a line left over, so he could put in this extra information and not charge the customer anything more. When you can, you might just as well give him good measure for his money, Ted decided, and rewrote the ad. He took it back to the printing room and explained where it was to go, and how the last short paragraph in the story above would have to come out.

"Hold on, Ted," said Mr. White, "and I'll have a proof on it for you in a minute."

He did, and it came out all right.

"Well, that's it, then, put her to bed," said Ted with a great deal of satisfaction, for it was the first time he had ever been able to make that welcome announcement.

He looked at the clock. It was just five minutes to twelve. They were running right on schedule. He went out for lunch.

5.

Troubles Pile Up

AS SHE HAD promised, Ted's mother called later that afternoon, and the news she had for him was not good.

"When I arrived there, Ted, I found Miss Monroe hadn't even consulted a doctor. As soon as I saw how ill she was, I insisted that a doctor be called. He came at once, and after a short check ordered her to the hospital."

"What's the trouble?" Ted inquired.

"It appears to be appendicitis. She's had some trouble along that line before."

"Is she going to be operated upon?"

"That's the way it looks. I think she's reconciled to the operation. The thing she objects to is that she will be leaving the newspaper in the lurch. She wants to postpone it for a while if she can."

"Tell her not to be silly. If she needs the operation, now's as good a time as any. We'll be able to run things here for a while without her."

"All right, Ted, I'll add my small voice to the doctor's, for whatever it may be worth, and let you know. How are you and Carl getting along?"

"I'll get along with him somehow," said Ted doggedly, "even if I have to chew nails."

Although the news wasn't good, it wasn't so bad as it might

have been, and the chances were that Miss Monroe would be back on the job in a week or two. Meanwhile, if he got into difficulties it would probably be possible for him to consult her about it. Somehow he felt a little relieved, now that he knew how matters stood and what was expected of him.

Besides, he had more than a little confidence in his ability to meet a challenge of this kind. In addition to serving on the school newspaper and acting as high-school correspondent for the *Town Crier*, he had spent much of his spare time for the last year or two around the office. And then there was Ronald, whose enthusiasm for the newspaper profession filled his conversation and eventually aroused the same spark in Ted. And if Ted was short on practical experience, his energy and enthusiasm might help fill the gap.

Fortunately for Ted there was nothing he had to do for the paper once it had been "put to bed." In the back room the presses were already rolling. Their part-time circulation manager, Mr. Oliver, would come in that evening and spend most of the night taking care of the mailing and the bundling of papers for the home carriers.

Therefore, Ted could focus his whole attention on the next issue. He saw at once that it was going to be a much more difficult task than anything he had faced so far. It would be up to him to decide which items of news were of most importance—no doubt, with some advice from Carl Allison—how they should be written up, and to assign them their proper place in the paper.

How did a small-town newspaper, without a wire service, get its news, anyway? Mr. Dobson kept an assignment book somewhere in his desk, and Ted looked through the drawers until he found it. There was a double page for each issue of the paper, and in it the editor had listed every tip he had for a news story that might be suitable. The pages for the next issue were nearly filled, but there were entries for later dates, too—some of them still months away. These tips came from all sorts of places—from people the editor had talked to, stories or tips people had phoned in, some came from letters, some consisted of publicity releases from various organizations or branches of government, some the editor had evidently thought of himself. Most of the local churches, clubs, and other organizations had a publicity secretary whose job was to inform the newspaper of any items which might be newsworthy. People who were merely seeking publicity for their own organizations were not paid by the newspaper. But the newspaper had a string of correspondents in outlying territories who gathered the local items in their communities, and these people received regular space rates —just as Ted had while he was serving as high-school correspondent.

Ted looked through some of the items Mr. Dobson had listed. Even if nothing new came in, they ought to have plenty to go on for the coming issue. Carl Allison would cover the outside reporting angle, of course, while he would have the less interesting job of sitting in the office and keeping the wheels turning.

But news stories were only part of the problem. Equal in volume, if not in wordage, would be the advertising, and here was a field where Ted realized he might easily find himself at sea. He knew that some businesses ran the same ad—or business card—every week. Others contracted for the same space every week but always changed their copy. And then there were the transient advertisers, who advertised in only one issue, or sometimes two or three, or only on special occasions. Though he knew about the regulars, he would have to check into the others.

He found an advertising book in which Miss Monroe had marked the ads that were to be held over. He wondered if some of the transients would want to take out new ads, and he knew he would have to watch these carefully, for he didn't want to lose any advertising revenue if he could help it. If the copy didn't come in, he might have to telephone each one, and if his experience on the school paper was any indication, he might have to telephone several times to those who showed indecision. But when it came to matters of type size and face, arrangements, cuts, or drawings, Ted knew he was out of his depth and was thankful that he could rely on Mr. White for information along these lines.

Besides news and advertising, the *Town Crier* carried several regular columns, one on homemaking and another a political column, written by local people, and he knew these would come in on time. Another column consisted of little jokes, sayings, and poems contributed by readers, and here Ted realized it would be up to him to make the best possible choices. The letters-to-the-editor column would also require selection. Pictures were no problem, for the paper could handle very few and usually had many more contributed than it could use. When Carl wanted a picture to accompany a story he usually arranged with a local photographer to take it for him.

Editorials offered a more serious problem. Ted had read the paper for so many years, and knew Mr. Dobson so well, that he felt he had a pretty good idea of the things Mr. Dobson believed in. Still, Mr. Dobson was an experienced, fighting editor while he was merely a raw cub, and even when the two happened to believe in the same things, Ted knew he couldn't hope to imitate the editor's hard, uncompromising style. No, he decided, he didn't feel he wanted to write any editorials; he couldn't take a chance on committing the newspaper in this fashion. However, a solution occurred to him.

The *Town Crier* was on an exchange basis with many other small newspapers in the state, and even a few out of the state. Occasionally Mr. Dobson reprinted an editorial from one of these other papers, assigning due credit, of course. Maybe he could fill the whole editorial column with writings from other sources. That wouldn't be a wise thing as a steady diet, but it might prove interesting for a while, and the readers, knowing of Mr. Dobson's accident, would understand the reason for it.

The size of the newspaper was another matter to consider. Generally it consisted of ten pages, but sometimes it ran to twelve when advertising was heavy. Just now, in the summer months, advertising was running light, and Ted seriously considered the advisability of cutting back to eight pages. That might be better than attempting to do too much and making a hash of it. He'd have to ask Miss Monroe about it when he saw her.

Unexpectedly Carl Allison came in late in the afternoon and seemed in a more amiable mood than was usual for him. Probably his stories had gone very well during the day, Ted decided.

"Well, how'd you make out, Ted?" asked Carl cheerfully. "Get my story in all right?"

"Yes, I guess so," Ted replied a little cautiously, still not ready to accept Carl's overtures too eagerly. "You can see the proof if you want to."

"Oh, don't bother. I've got a couple stories I want to type up before five." Ted explained about Miss Monroe's operation, but Carl only shook his head with sympathy. He sat down at the typing table, which Ted had shoved back into its original position once he had learned that Miss Monroe wasn't coming in. Ted found it more convenient from every angle to establish himself at her desk.

"Any last-minute changes?" Carl inquired.

"No, hardly anything. Just an ad came in."

"What kind of ad?"

"Classified—lost-and-found."

"Somebody telephone it in? I hope you called back to verify it."

"No, why should I?"

"Good heavens!" Carl exploded, more like his old self again. "Where did you learn your journalism? Don't you know lots of people phone in ads as a joke on their friends, or on somebody they don't like? They hope to flood him with nuisance calls. In the newspaper business you *never* believe anything you hear over the telephone, unless you're sure who's calling."

"It wasn't any joke this time," said Ted nonchalantly. "He didn't even list a phone number. He rented a box."

Carl spun about in his chair. "A box number for a lost-and-found? What's the big idea? I never heard of such a thing. It's about ten times easier to get people to make a phone call than it is to get them to write a letter."

"He said it was more convenient for him. Maybe he wasn't very hopeful about getting it back anyway."

"Did you get his name and address?"

"I got his name and telephone number, and as long as we've got the telephone number we can always get the address from the telephone company, if we have to. What's the difference, anyway? For a buck seventy-five we ought to be able to trust a man."

"Well, maybe, but it sounds pretty fishy to me. If I were you I'd call him back, just to make sure."

"And tell him what?"

"Read the ad to him and ask him if it sounds all right. It's too late now to make any changes, but if he's not a newspaperman he probably won't know the difference."

It seemed like a lot of fuss over nothing, but Ted decided he might as well call anyway, not so much to please Carl, but to prove to Carl he was wrong. He dialed the number, and after a couple of rings Mr. Denning answered.

"This is Ted Wilford at the *Town Crier* office. I thought you might like me to read your ad to you, and see if it sounds all right."

"That hardly sounds necessary. But as long as you've called, go ahead."

Ted read it to him, and Mr. Denning did not sound very well pleased. "I told you I changed my mind about that 'red leather' and 'zipper.' There isn't any need to describe it that exactly."

"I had the space to spare, so I put it in anyway. It won't cost anything extra."

"Well—I suppose it doesn't hurt anything." Mr. Denning's acceptance still sounded grudging. "Thanks for calling, and I'll be in tomorrow to pay for the ad, as I promised." He hung up.

"Nothing phony about it," Ted informed Carl. "It's his ad, all right. There can't be any question about his identity."

"O.K., O.K.," said Carl disinterestedly, and returned to his typing.

Whether the story he was writing was finished or not, Carl always left promptly at five o'clock. Ted hung around a little longer, for he had some odds and ends to clean up. Besides, he was still hoping to hear from his mother. Finally the telephone did ring.

"It's definitely appendicitis," his mother reported, "and though it isn't exactly an emergency, she's consented to the operation. But as long as it isn't an emergency, she felt she'd like to go back to her home town, where she could be with her family."

"Sure, that's nice," said Ted, a little dully, for now he realized that Miss Monroe wasn't going to be available to advise him, as he had hoped. Now the responsibility for the whole paper was squarely on his—and Carl's—shoulders.

6.

A Treaty of Peace

WHEN CARL came bouncing in the next morning, it was clear even before he opened his mouth that he was angry over something.

"So the boy wonder editor did it again," he exclaimed bitterly.

"Did what?" asked Ted, puzzled.

"Didn't you read the *Town Crier* this morning?"

"Of course I read it," said Ted, who had looked it over rather hastily that morning.

"And you didn't see anything wrong?"

"Not that I noticed."

"Then you didn't see that the boy wonder had the park commissioner electing the president of the P.T.A., and the P.T.A. leasing the fair grounds for the season. It was so glaring it's a wonder it didn't leap out and snap you on the nose."

"Where—I don't believe it," Ted retorted, but reached for a copy of the paper. For a moment he still didn't believe it—and then it suddenly came to him. The headlines over the two stories had been interchanged.

He was almost stunned. Getting out a newspaper is always a battle against time, so that putting out a perfect paper is nearly impossible. Copyreaders soon grow philosophical about the jumbled line that appears in print, the lines interchanged, or the story shortened until it doesn't make sense. But because headlines are so conspicuous, they never quite get reconciled to errors there. Yet it is precisely because headlines are in such large type and the errors so obvious, and because they are so often written at a later time when they may not be proofread, that some glaring errors occasionally occur.

Still Ted could hardly believe it. He had pasted on the headlines so carefully, following Miss Monroe's guides exactly. He looked up the dummy, and then he saw what must have happened. The stories were of about equal length, and evidently for some reason Miss Monroe had decided to reverse their locations but had not reversed the penciled-in headlines above. Then when Ted cut out the headlines he had pasted them carefully over the pencil headlines, without comparing them with the stories beneath. Of course Miss Monroe would have caught it had she been there, and so would Ted if he had known more about what to watch for.

It wasn't a matter of life or death, and probably the readers who noticed it would get a little laugh out of it and then give it no more thought. Still, it is the kind of error that makes a newspaperman wince. There wasn't anything Ted could say. It was his boner, all right, and any attempt to excuse it would only arouse Carl's further derision.

"Look, Carl," he said patiently, "I know that for some reason you and I seem to rub each other the wrong way. But it looks like we're stuck with each other for a while, whether we like it or not. So why don't we sign a treaty of peace—at least until Miss Monroe gets back?"

Getting out the paper alone was going to be tough enough, without complicating the picture by constant bickering, and Carl could see that.

"All right, Ted," he agreed grudgingly. "You tend to the

office, and I'll handle the outside assignments, and maybe we'll be able to stay out of each other's way. Heaven knows we'll both have enough to do. I've got not only my own assignments to handle, but Miss Monroe and Mr. Dobson often went out on stories, too, and I'll have to cover their fields."

Ted got out Mr. Dobson's assignment book, and they went over the stories he had listed. Carl told him which stories he was handling, and what he was doing about them. He also had leads on a couple of stories Mr. Dobson hadn't listed, and he was following these up, too. Some of the other stories could probably be handled right from the office, with perhaps only a phone call or two, and Ted would take care of these.

After Carl left, Ted set about planning the next issue. The first thing, he thought, was to begin setting up the dummy, but here he was stymied because he didn't know enough about the advertising layout. He huddled with Mr. White, and they pored over the advertising book. Miss Monroe was a neat, methodical person, but some of the notations she made were a mystery. However, between them they were able to figure almost everything out, and when they were finished Ted had a list of advertisers to telephone to see if they wanted to renew.

Fortunately he was interrupted by few incoming telephone calls. Several people called to inquire about Mr. Dobson's condition, and as Ted had telephoned the hospital before leaving home, he was able to say that Mr. Dobson's condition was satisfactory, but he was still unable to receive visitors.

Then Ted got busy working down the list of advertisers. He was either very persuasive, or very lucky, for most of the advertisers decided to renew. He was especially gratified about this because he knew he couldn't go out and solicit new business, the way Mr. Dobson did, but at least they were holding on to most of their old business.

By late morning Ted was able to block out the better part of the advertising on the dummy—they would attempt only eight pages, he decided—and he now had an idea how much news space he was going to have. His talk with Carl had helped him assess the value of the news stories, and he was already beginning to plan where he would put them and how much space they would occupy.

After lunch he tackled the big stack of mail that had piled up. In Ronald's fashion, he dropped a substantial part of it in the wastebasket, made another pile that required attention, and pushed aside a third that was available for further reference if he needed it.

The stories from the out-of-town correspondents were beginning to come in. These were experienced writers with a good idea of their space allotments, and their neatly typed copy could go directly to the printer with little editing. Ted was glad to see this, for if he had had to type everything going into the paper, even an eight-page issue, it would have been more than he could handle. Some of the advertising, too, was held over, and the new, big display ads involved large type, and a lot of space, with very little copy. Carl would type his own stories. And when it came to selecting letters to the editor for publication, other considerations being equal, Ted decided to give preference to those which were short, well written, and typed so that they, too, could go straight to the printer. The editorials he selected from other papers could be clipped out so they would not have to be typed. The rest of it he would have to manage somehow.

The stories from publicity secretaries were less professional. Often they ran to half a column or more, and Ted knew he would have to cut them to two or three short paragraphs, for if time is one enemy of newspapermen, space is the other.

A visitor Ted had been expecting came in during the afternoon. He was a man of average height, slender, wearing glasses, and a small, neat mustache.

"I'm Harold Denning," he introduced himself. "I placed an ad about a lost notebook."

"Oh, yes, Mr. Denning. I was expecting you."

"Worried about your money?" said the man with a laugh, reaching for his wallet. "How much is it?"

Ted told him, he paid it, and received a receipt.

"I don't suppose there are any answers yet?"

"No, but it's a little too early to expect that."

"I suppose so. The truth is that I'm not really expecting an answer at all. People no longer seem to hold to the same standards of honesty that my generation was taught when we were little. On the other hand, since the papers would be useless to the finder, it may be that I'll be hearing yet. I'll be in again in a day or two to check."

"I hope you get it," Ted answered. "We like to think that our advertising pays off. If it does come in, I could give you a ring."

"Oh, I doubt that you'd reach me, as I'm seldom home, and there's no one else there. Tell you what we can do. I've got some stamps here." He took them from his wallet. "If it comes in, you can mail it to me. There's nothing very urgent about it. I'd just like to have it back."

When Mr. Denning had gone, Ted returned to his work. He felt that he had made a good deal of progress, not only in what he had accomplished, but in learning how to handle the job.

Late in the day Nelson stopped in.

"I just thought I'd drop in and see how the boy editor is getting along." He grinned. Although he had unconsciously used almost the same expression Carl had used, Ted didn't mind it coming from his best friend.

"Holding down the fort so far."

Nelson looked around in wonder at the stacks of papers and the general note of mild confusion. "A good thing this isn't my job. I wouldn't be able to make head or tail out of this mess. Anything I can help you with?" He sank back into a chair, as though he wasn't eager to do very much.

"No, I can't think of anything." If he were in need of muscles, Ted knew that Nelson would be the first person he would turn to, but clerical work with its endless details was a different matter. Anyway, things were confused enough without getting another finger in the pie.

"Then don't let me bother you," Nelson went on. "I knew you'd be busy, but I didn't have anything else to do and it's getting on toward quitting time, so I thought maybe you'd like a lift home."

"Thanks," said Ted gratefully.

They were almost ready to close up when a woman came in, her manner hesitant. She was carrying a package in her hands, and at sight of it Ted's interest immediately perked up.

"Is this the *Town Crier* office?" she asked, although the name on the window was very clear.

"Yes, it is," Ted replied, "and I'm Ted Wilford. Can I help you?"

She opened a copy of that morning's paper and turned to the classified ads.

"It says here that there was a package containing a red leather notebook lost on the train between Stanton and Forestdale. This sounds like the one I found."

She opened the parcel and drew out the notebook. It was just as Mr. Denning had described it, with a zipper running around the edge. In addition, the initials H.D. were embossed on the cover.

"Yes, that seems to be it," Ted responded, feeling well pleased. "You say you found it on the train?"

"Yes. Well, I didn't exactly find it—but I was tired, and

there was so much confusion. I didn't turn it over to the station manager because I didn't find it till I was home, and then I wasn't exactly sure I'd found it on the train. I'd done some early-morning shopping in Stanton and thought perhaps I'd picked it up in the store with my other parcels."

She seemed a little confused, but Ted did not press her for the details. This was obviously the package Mr. Denning had lost, and as long as it was found again, what difference did the details make?

"I know Mr. Denning will be very pleased. As you know there was mention of a reward."

"Oh, I don't want any reward," said the woman quickly. "I'm sure it was my fault, probably, and I thought I might be blamed for it. I'm just glad the real owner will get it back."

But at Ted's urging she gave her name as Mrs. Conway, and an address in Stanton, with another address in Brightsville, a small community farther down the line, where she said she'd be staying for a while.

"But be sure and tell him I don't want any reward, and that I didn't mean to take it," she called to Ted as she left.

Nelson had arisen and came over to Ted's side, where they both examined the notebook. They had never seen anything quite like it. The notebook was unusual in that the handle of the zipper was folded over into a lock, so that it was impossible to examine the contents without breaking the lock.

"And a good thing for us," Nelson pointed out, "for then he can't claim anybody tampered with the contents."

However, it looked very official and important—more important, Ted suspected, than Mr. Denning had let on to him.

"But I wonder why he didn't mention the initials on the cover?" Ted speculated. "That would have been a sure means of identifying it."

"Probably forgot," said Nelson, stretching lazily. "Well, what do we do now?"

"I'd sort of like to get it back to him in a hurry," said Ted slowly, "just to show him the kind of efficient service we give our advertisers—even though he said it wasn't very urgent. He asked me to mail it to him, but I wonder if we couldn't drive out and leave it at his house right now."

"All right by me," Nelson agreed. "Where does he live?"

Ted had the address written down, and showed it to Nelson.

"Ouch! That's ten miles out of town," Nelson exclaimed.

"So far? Well, I suppose I could mail it—"

"Oh, I don't mind a little drive before supper. I only hope you got enough for the ad to make it worth while."

"No, I can't say we did," Ted responded, stopping only long enough to gather together a few papers he wanted to take home and to lock the door before following Nelson to the curb.

Not owning a car of his own, Ted was not too familiar with all the byroads around Forestdale, but Nelson thought he knew where the place was.

"Not farms, if I remember right," he said, "but sort of estates—wealthy people who want to get away from it all."

"He didn't look particularly wealthy," Ted recollected, "but then you never can tell."

It was a pleasant drive after a long, hot day at the office, and Ted relaxed as they talked of other things. Nelson did not have a summer job, and was undecided whether he was going to try to get one.

"We'll be counseling at the Y camp later," he reminded Ted, "and then it'll be almost time for college. Besides, I wasn't very anxious to get a job before the senior picnic. You're going, aren't you, Ted?"

"Oh, I suppose so. Miss Monroe ought to be back by then."

"You feel kind of funny, being out of school, don't you?"

"Funny how?"

"Oh, I don't know—as though you're almost grown up, but you're still not quite sure about it."

"All I know is I'm feeling bushed," Ted answered practically.

They turned off the main highway, into a less-traveled road. Ted soon saw that Nelson was right—this was a section of fine homes, not in the millionaire class but well above average.

"We're pretty far out from town," Ted observed. "I didn't think our local telephone company extended this far, but Mr. Denning had a Forestdale number."

"It must. It's not a big company as utilities go, but it covers a pretty big area. Now how the devil do these numbers run, anyway?"

Most of the homes were set well back from the road but had rural-style mailboxes in front of them. Each box had a large number painted on it, and they soon discovered the numbers ran consecutively downward. The number Mr. Denning had given could not be far off, and presently they came to it. Nelson turned up the drive.

This was a home comparable to the others, partly hidden behind twin maple trees that stood on either side of a curving concrete walk leading down to the mailbox. The spacious, well-kept lawn, the long drive, and the elegance of the house itself all added to Ted's growing belief that somehow this notebook he was carrying was of far more importance than Mr. Denning had indicated to him. He was glad now they had decided to deliver it in person.

Getting out of the car, they walked toward the house. The blinds were closed, and there was a stillness that seemed unusual to their ears, used to the noises of town, school, and traffic. Moreover, there didn't seem to be anyone about.

"He said there might not be anybody home," Ted remembered.

"I wonder why a man who lives all alone would want a house as big as this one?" Nelson speculated.

"He might not live alone. Maybe everyone's away."

"But you'd think in a house this big there'd be servants, wouldn't you? Somebody ought to be around."

There was no time for further comment, as Ted gave the doorbell a steady ring. They waited in silence for a minute, but there was no answer. Ted rang again, longer than before, and then they waited another minute without results.

"There ought to be somebody here," Ted muttered. "The door doesn't seem to be quite closed."

But Nelson was not at his side. He was pacing back and forth across the veranda, when he stopped to look into one of the windows.

"Hey, Ted—come over here a minute. Here's something strange."

Ted walked over to the window. He didn't quite like the idea of snooping, but neither could he figure out what was going on. If this notebook really was valuable, it was his duty to get as much background on the matter as he could. He looked in, then he, too, exclaimed:

"Why, it's empty! There's nothing here!"

7.

The Ghostly Telephone

"IT'S JUST about the emptiest house I've ever seen," Nelson remarked. "There isn't a stick of furniture anywhere in sight."

"Now I wonder why in thunderation Mr. Denning gave me the address of an empty house?" Ted pondered.

"What are you going to do, leave the package here?"

"Not on your sweet life," said Ted firmly. "Apparently I've got hold of something somebody wants, and if Mr. Denning wishes to claim it he'll have to explain a few things to me."

"I don't think that door's locked. Could we go in, or would that be burglary?"

"No, I don't think it would be burglary. That's breaking into an occupied house after dark. It isn't after dark, and the house isn't occupied, and we aren't breaking in. However, I don't think we've got anything to gain from entering an empty house, and if worst came to worst we might have a little trouble explaining what we're doing. Let's go."

With some reluctance they started to walk back toward the car. Before they reached the vehicle, they stopped as a ringing sound came to their ears.

"A telephone!" said Nelson, puzzled. "Where's it coming from?"

"From the house, of course. Where else could it come from?"

"But why's a telephone ringing in an empty house?"

"I don't know, but I'm going to try to find out. Come on."

"I thought you said we didn't have any business in there," Nelson muttered.

"We do now," said Ted briefly, leading the way.

The door was not locked and opened easily at their touch. It took them a few moments longer, in those spacious rooms, to locate the telephone, still ringing loudly, and they half-expected it might stop ringing before they could get there. However, they located it at last in a little alcove off what they thought to be the dining room, and the line was still alive as Ted put the receiver to his ear.

"Hello," he answered cautiously.

"Is this Ted Wilford?" came from a rather indistinct man's voice.

"Yes, it is," said Ted in some surprise.

"Oh, Ted, I'm glad I caught you." The man sounded very relieved, and as his voice was now stronger, Ted was able to recognize it. "Ted, this is Harold Denning. I called your office, and they told me you'd left, so I thought I just might be able to catch you out there." His voice became eager. "Did you get the notebook?"

"Yes, I guess we did," Ted answered.

"A large red notebook, with a zipper that locks? The initials H.D. on the cover?"

"That about describes it. How come you didn't tell me about the initials before? That would have identified it for sure."

The man laughed, obviously much relieved that his package had been found. "I thought I'd better hold back part of the description so I could prove it was mine if it was found. I had another reason, though. I didn't want to describe it too well in the ad because I didn't want any of my friends to find out what a stupid thing I'd done."

"Then it is pretty valuable?" Ted questioned.

"Yes, it's very important to me, though, as I said before, it wouldn't mean much to the finder. Well, I suppose there is a matter of the reward involved. If you'd care to give me the name of the finder, I'll see that he receives some suitable recompense."

"She said she didn't want any reward. She sort of thought it was her fault for getting it mixed up."

"I doubt that," said the man, laughing once more. "Things were pretty hectic around the station yesterday morning. It was probably more my fault than hers. However, I'll do whatever you think best."

"I'd drop it," Ted advised him. "You'd only embarrass her if you tried to reward her."

"Well, all right," the man agreed.

"What about this house out here?" Ted inquired. "You told us you lived here, and now we find the house is empty."

"Oh, I suppose I should have explained that to you, although I didn't think you'd be coming out. You see, I've just bought the house. I was expecting my van of furniture to arrive yesterday, but it was delayed on the road, and I've just had word that it's due to get there this evening. Of course I expected to be in there before this. I even ordered the utilities turned on. The telephone's connected, as you see. Can you tell me if the electricity is on yet?"

"I don't know, but the doorbell rang."

"I believe that's on a battery, not on a transformer. Would you try the lights, please?"

Ted motioned to Nelson to try a switch, and he did, but there was no response.

"No, there's no electricity."

"Oh, well," the man sighed, "I suppose we'll be able to work all right by lantern. I left the door unlocked for the utility men."

Ted looked at the telephone cradle. The number said Forestdale 8106. Then this was the number he had telephoned yesterday, and Mr. Denning must have been here.

"Then you were out here yesterday when I called?" he asked.

"Oh, yes, I was out there picking up a little, and waiting for my furniture. Then I learned that it wasn't coming, so I returned to the hotel where I've been staying."

"Oh," said Ted, a little disappointed that the mystery could be so easily explained.

"Well, I suppose there's still the question of my picking up the notebook," Mr. Denning continued.

"We can drop it off at the hotel, if you want us to," Ted offered.

"No, you'd probably miss me. I'm checking out of my room. My furniture was promised definitely for tonight, so I'll just come out and wait for it. I'll tell you what, Ted. On the other side of the room you'll see a window seat, and below it are three drawers. Suppose you put it in the middle drawer, and I'll be able to pick it up when I get there. It should be safe enough there for a couple of hours."

"Well, all right, if that's how you want it," Ted agreed.

"Yes, I think that'll do. And I must say this is pretty good service for an ad in a country newspaper, and I appreciate your helping out the way you have, too. Are you sure I can't reward you in some way?"

"No, it's all part of our service."

"Well, all right, then, and thanks very much, Ted. This means more to me than you'll ever know. Good-by."

"Good-by," and Ted replaced the receiver. "He wants me to leave it in the drawer over there," he explained to Nelson.

"Are you going to?"

"Why not? It's his notebook, and it's up to him to decide what he wants done with it."

"You're sure that was really Mr. Denning?" asked Nelson skeptically.

"Not a doubt of it in this world. I recognized the voice. Besides, he knew all about the ad and the notebook. It's his notebook, he advertised for it, it's got his initials on it. And this must be his house, all right. The telephone number is the same, and he knew just where those drawers are located. So I guess that's all there is to it." He pulled open the middle drawer, thrust the notebook in, and closed it once more, a little shower of dust greeting these maneuvers.

"I wonder how he happened to call you here?"

"He said he called the office, and Mr. White must have told him where we were."

"Did Mr. White know?"

"He was there when Mrs. Conway came in, so he must have had a pretty good idea where we went."

"But I thought Mr. White was gone when we left."

"Probably just went out for a snack. You know our arrangement with him. He often picks up some extra money on the side by doing job printing after regular hours."

Nelson shrugged. As long as something could be explained, the details didn't interest him.

"But I still wonder what's in that notebook," he mused.

"And that's something we'll probably never know," said Ted blithely. "Mr. Denning didn't have much to say about that."

"Which means it must be pretty darned important," Nelson pointed out, and Ted grinned.

"Probably is, or it wouldn't have been in a locked notebook. You weren't thinking of breaking in, were you?"

"No, but I kind of wish Mrs. Conway had."

Nelson was rather piqued, for he had a strong sense of curiosity which hadn't been completely satisfied. Ted's curiosity was equally strong, but it didn't bother him particularly if it couldn't be entirely satisfied. Instead, it gave him something to speculate on. Besides, a newspaperman always has this feeling over a big story. He has his story, the part that will interest his readers is published, but a few threads are left over that the reporter knows he will never pick up again. So it was this time, even though this wasn't really a story.

Nelson looked around with frank interest. "Something kind of spooky about an empty house, even in the daylight, isn't there?"

"Guess so," Ted agreed, for their footsteps sounded harsh on the bare hardwood floors and their voices echoed through the empty rooms. Unconsciously they had been talking in more subdued tones than normally. "The light creeping through the blinds seems funny, and I suppose there ought to be cobwebs, though I don't see any."

"As long as you're sure we're not burglars, why don't we look it over?" Nelson suggested.

"What for?"

"Oh, I don't know—just sort of a queer feeling I've got about it. I'd like to be sure this house is really as empty as it seems."

Ted looked at his watch. It was just five minutes after five. They had plenty of time before supper, if they wanted to look around.

"Oh, all right," he consented. "Anyway, maybe we'll want to buy a house like this someday."

"Not on army pay," Nelson returned.

They walked slowly around the lower floor, admiring many of the house's fine features including the expensive carvings on the rails, but finding some fault, too, with the design.

"Pantries are out of date," said Nelson scornfully, "and the study is too close to the front room. Now when I get *my* house—"

"Then you can plan it the way you want it." Ted laughed.

They paused in front of the staircase. "Going upstairs?" Nelson inquired.

"We've gone this far, we might as well, if you really want to."

They went upstairs, not at all fearfully, although the rooms above were much darker than those below. However, there was nothing to be afraid of, unless emptiness itself is a cause for alarm, for there was nothing in any of the rooms above. Nelson even opened all the closet doors, but except for a couple of coat hangers, there was nothing to show that the rooms had ever been occupied.

"I wonder if there's an attic," said Nelson, glancing around, but if there was, they were unable to find the way to reach it.

"I don't think so. These are dormer windows, and that usually means this is the top floor. Might be some empty space in these walls, though."

Downstairs once more, taking what was apparently the servants' stairway in the rear, Nelson began looking around for the cellarway.

"Still not satisfied?" asked Ted with some amusement. "What are you after, hunting for rats?"

"No, thank you. I think I can get along without rats very well."

"What's the matter with rats?" asked Ted. "They're friendly enough when you understand them."

"I'm not sure they understand *me*," Nelson replied.

He found the stairway, and they made their way down in the nearly pitch dark. The recent inhabitants had left some traces here, in the form of a few packing boxes, wastepaper, and cardboard, but once again there was really nothing for them to see, although Nelson opened the doors into the fruit cellars just to make sure. They returned upstairs, Nelson somewhat disappointed.

"You know something," he remarked, as they made their way outside into the now bright sunshine, "I've a feeling that Mr. Denning didn't want to see you again."

"Didn't want to see me? Why?"

"Dunno. But maybe he just didn't want to pay any reward, and he felt he'd have to if he saw you."

"How cheesy can you get for a few bucks?"

"How do you know it's only a few bucks? Maybe that notebook's really worth a lot of money, and if you knew what was in it, you'd expect a reward of perhaps a thousand dollars. That's worth getting out of."

"Sure, and maybe all it's got in it are a few insurance policies that would be hard to replace."

Imagination was all right, and Ted occasionally liked to indulge in flights of fancy, but he was sorry to admit that in this case there wasn't very much room for imagination. It all sounded very practical and simple—someone's property lost, the owner very worried then very pleased when it is finally returned—all except for a telephone ringing in an empty house.

"I suppose you're right," Nelson agreed regretfully. What had started out as a promising adventure seemed to have ended on a flat note. "The finder of that notebook might have had a problem, though. There was no identification on the outside, and he might be undecided whether he ought to break the lock open or not. Maybe that was the reason Mr. Denning was so anxious to get an ad in the paper."

"I wonder if you could be right about what's in that notebook," said Ted thoughtfully. "It doesn't exactly seem the sort of thing in which a man would carry around insurance policies and things like that, does it? So far Mr. Denning has been pretty cagey about not telling us exactly what was in there. I don't know, but to me that notebook suggests some sort of business deal—you know, contracts, confidential price lists, and things like that. Maybe he was very anxious that his competitors shouldn't get hold of it."

"Well, it's out of our hands now, anyway," Nelson responded with a gesture of dismissal.

"Maybe—at least I hope so." Ted was still not too pleased with the way things had gone. "But supposing that notebook is valuable, I don't quite like the idea of leaving it in an empty house. How do we know who might come along and pick it up?"

"He told you to leave it, didn't he? What else could you do?"

"That's true enough. It's his notebook, and I had to follow his suggestions. But maybe we put him on the spot. He knew we were out at the empty house. He didn't want us to hang on to the notebook because we might get curious and break it open, especially if we thought it was valuable. And maybe you're right, he wasn't anxious to meet me again, and perhaps have me ask him some more questions about the notebook. Leaving it at the empty house was the first thing he could think of on the spur of the moment."

"Anyway, there's nobody around," said Nelson, glancing carefully in all directions, "and I don't think anybody could have followed us out from town. If that notebook is valuable, you can be sure Mr. Denning will be hotfooting it out here just as fast as he can make it. You weren't thinking of going back and getting the notebook, were you?"

"No, I guess not," said Ted slowly. "I promised, and I can't see any real reason for breaking my promise. I doubt if anyone else will have the chance to pick it up, but if it did happen to get into the wrong hands, I'll be hearing about it in short order."

"That's for sure," said Nelson emphatically, but Ted didn't find his words very comforting as he followed him toward the car.

8.

A Rebuke from a V.A.I.P.

IN THE MORNING, still not satisfied with the events of the previous day, Ted looked up Mr. Denning's number in the telephone book, but it was not listed. On second thought, he realized that there was nothing strange about that. The book was nearly a year old, and if Mr. Denning was just moving into his new house, it couldn't possibly be listed. However, it did seem to prove that Mr. Denning was not a long-time resident of Forestdale. The town was a flourishing, growing community, and Ted did not know everyone by sight, especially the newcomers and transients who were constantly coming and going. Then there were many other persons who lived near Forestdale whom Ted did not know at all.

When Mr. White came in, Ted asked, "Was there a call for me yesterday afternoon after I'd left?"

"Yes, there was, Ted—a man, I don't recall his name."

"What did you tell him?"

"That you weren't here, and then he wanted to know if he could reach you at your home. I told him I didn't think you'd gone home, because you'd left early, and that usually meant you were out on some errand for the paper."

"What time did he call?"

"About ten minutes after five, I think it was. The phone was ringing as I came in the office door."

Ordinarily Mr. White left at four-thirty, and the office

closed at five. Then, if Mr. White intended to work in the evening, he generally returned about five o'clock. Yesterday, because of his desire to return the notebook, Ted had left with Nelson at a little after four-thirty, taking along some work to finish at home to ease his conscience. Ted's watch was synchronized with the electric clock in the office, and since he had talked to Mr. Denning at about five o'clock, he supposed that Mr. Denning must have called the office earlier than Mr. White had said. The only other explanation was that Mr. Denning must have called Ted at the empty house *first*, and then called the office, and that didn't make any sense, did it? If Mr. Denning hadn't called the office first, how would he have known Ted was out at the empty house? Probably Mr. White was wrong about the time. Maybe his own watch was wrong, and he hadn't checked with the office clock. This might easily happen if he was in a hurry to answer the telephone.

Everything was probably all right, and it was quite likely he'd never hear anything about Mr. Denning again, Ted decided, as he turned to his work. Later Carl came in, much of his amiability of the previous day still remaining, and they had a friendly discussion of their plans for the day. However, it seemed to Ted that Carl still held a scornful, condescending attitude toward him, but was trying to conceal it.

Just as Carl was preparing to leave, a man came into the office. He was big and heavy, and apparently very much in a hurry. The shove he gave the office door was hardly gentle, and his manner was blustering.

"Who's in charge here?" he demanded, turning first toward Ted, who was occupying the front desk, and then to Carl as the older of the two.

"I suppose you might say I am," Carl answered, "at least for the moment. What can I do for you, Mr.—you're Mr. Montague, aren't you?"

"That's right." The man seemed to have hard work containing himself. "I'm Cyril P. Montague, the state auditor."

"Well, how can I help you?" asked Carl calmly, as though having such a prominent visitor in their small office was a common occurrence. Clearly, Carl wasn't at all impressed, or was at least trying to pretend he wasn't, which only seemed to infuriate their visitor the more.

"I came here to inquire about an advertisement in yesterday's paper—in the lost-and-found column—concerning a red leather notebook with a zipper. Can you tell me whether it has been turned in yet?"

Carl, who did not know of the trip out to the deserted house, referred the inquiry to Ted. Unexpectedly, Ted found his heart beating a little faster. Then he hadn't heard the end of Mr. Denning and the notebook even yet! Before answering, he asked cautiously:

"Could you describe the notebook a little more thoroughly?"

"Certainly I could. It was a somewhat unusual notebook in that the zipper on it could be locked, thus insuring privacy from casual snoopers. And it had the initials H.D. on the cover. Well, did you find it or didn't you?"

"Yes, it was turned in yesterday afternoon by the finder."

"Good. Then let me have it, please. Oh, it's my notebook, all right." He waved a small metallic object in the air. "This is the key that fits it. Furthermore, I can describe the contents to you in detail. Is that sufficient? Now may I see the notebook?"

"I'm sorry," Ted stammered, "but I've already returned it to the owner—I mean, to the person I *thought* was the owner. He was the man who ran the advertisement—"

"You mean I'm not in time? But if the notebook was turned in only yesterday afternoon, and I rushed down here the first thing this morning, as soon as this advertisement was brought to my attention—I telephoned first but your office apparently wasn't open yet—why isn't the notebook here? Surely the man who advertised couldn't have timed it that closely."

"I took it out to him yesterday afternoon," Ted explained. "He'd left his address with me."

"You say he left his address with you? This sounds incredible, but maybe it'll be some help after all. Where does he live?"

"I can give it to you, but I don't know whether you'll find him," said Ted unhappily. "It was an empty house."

"What! You mean to say you delivered this notebook to a man in an empty house? This is the most unbelievable thing I've ever heard of—although no more than one might expect from a hick country paper, I suppose."

Carl's eyes had also narrowed. "How did you happen to leave it at an empty house, Ted?"

Much chagrined, Ted explained about his errand with Nelson the previous afternoon. Although they understood what he had done, neither Carl nor Mr. Montague seemed able to appreciate why he had done it.

"This beats anything I've ever heard of before. This notebook was stolen from me, the thief calmly advertises for it in your paper, and you just as calmly return the stolen article to him. If there is a grain of common sense in this, it eludes me."

Unexpectedly Carl came to Ted's defense. "Now just a moment, Mr. Montague. This isn't a branch of the police department, and we're under no obligation to keep an eye out for stolen articles. A man advertised for a certain property he claimed he'd lost, the article was turned in, and we returned it to him. I don't see how you can hold us to blame for that. Was the theft reported to the police?"

"Well, no," Mr. Montague mumbled. "There were certain reasons why I thought it best to keep the theft as quiet as possible."

"Then," said Carl severely, "I think the blame is even more yours than ours. Had the theft been reported, the police would probably have been alert about it, the advertisement would have been noticed, and the matter reported to us."

"Well, I can't see that this is getting us anywhere," Mr. Montague replied. "The fact remains that a valuable property has been stolen, and turned over to the thief through a series of blunders, some of which I may have been somewhat responsible for myself. But nothing I did has matched the utter stupidity of returning an important document to an unknown man in an empty house."

"Perhaps if you'd tell us just what this document is," said Carl soothingly, "we'd have a better idea just how big a mistake has been made."

"As big as any you and I are ever likely to make," said Mr. Montague angrily. "May I speak off the record? I don't want any of this to get in the papers. Knowledge that the document has been lost could be equally as damaging as the theft itself."

"Sure, go ahead," Carl pledged. "We won't print anything about it until you release us, or until other papers get the story."

"The document concerns the new state thruway. You've heard of that, I suppose?" This last was spoken sarcastically, but both Carl and Ted nodded as though it were a serious question. "It gave the route that had been decided upon for the thruway, the engineers' estimates of costs, anticipated revenues, arrangements for financing, and so on. It is, in fact, a part of our next budget and would have been submitted to the next session of the Legislature along with the rest of the budget. That is why my office was concerned with it, although the report originated in the Highway Department. I need hardly point out to you that it is considered a grave breach of ethics to reveal any part of the budget ahead of time."

"The question of ethics aside," Carl picked up, "just who would get a monetary advantage from stealing the plans?"

"I should say that a good many people might stand to gain. As you know, there has been a great deal of controversy over the proposed route. If a thief knew exactly which route had been decided upon, he would be in a position to profit heavily by speculating in land along the right of way. While this is the most obvious advantage, it isn't the whole story, of course. Contractors, who were certain the highway was to be built and when, could corner essential materials. Banks and investment houses would be interested in the financing program. Everyone who pays taxes would be more or less interested in knowing our coming tax rate, and a few people would be able to turn this knowledge into a profit. For all these reasons a cloak of secrecy is thrown over the preparation of the budget until the time comes to release it to the public."

"How was the theft committed?" asked Ted, to whom this aspect of the affair was more appealing than considerations of profit.

"It was stolen from my apartment sometime over the weekend, but probably early Monday morning. That isn't my regular home. I maintain a small apartment near the capital in order to be available when the Legislature is in session. I was due to leave for a month's vacation, starting last Saturday. I locked the notebook in a steel cabinet in the small den of my apartment, and then my wife and I left for the seashore. On the way I received an urgent telegram from the governor, telling me of some new problem that had arisen in connection with the budget. My wife went on to the seashore, but I returned to the apartment. There I immediately found that the cabinet had been broken into, and the notebook was gone."

"Was there anyone who had access to the rooms—any servants?" Carl inquired.

"No—we don't maintain servants in the apartment. The

manager of the apartment house had a key, I presume. Other than that, no one was supposed to be admitted."

"What did you do when you discovered the theft?" Carl continued.

"What could I do? I had to tell the governor, of course, and he confidentially informed a few other high sources. We agreed that the best thing was to try to keep the matter hushed up for the time being. If word should leak out, there would be a tremendous outcry in the press. There would be a demand that the entire budget be released immediately, and unfortunately there are still a considerable number of obscure points about the budget, so that it *can't* be released just now. Then, too, there was the matter of catching the thief, and the hope that we might get him before he was able to profit on his knowledge. In all likelihood he didn't expect the theft to be discovered for a month, and so figured that he had a month to work it out. We decided if nothing concerning the theft was released to the press, it was quite possible we might catch the thief off guard, for he wouldn't be at such pains to cover his traces."

"You say the theft wasn't reported to the police. I suppose that you are making some effort to get the plans back?" asked Carl.

"I said that certain confidential sources had been informed," said the auditor stiffly. "I'm not at liberty to say more than that."

"Well, Mr. Montague, I sympathize with your plight, but I can't see how we could have acted much differently than we did. You wanted your secrecy, and because you insisted upon secrecy we weren't in a position to help you when we could have. You can have Mr. Denning's address, of course, but I doubt that it will do you any good. It obviously isn't his house, and he'll be miles away by now."

"It's that empty house that annoys me," the auditor griped.

"I suppose on a country newspaper, with inexperienced help, you can't expect anything more than that." He turned to Ted. "What grade are you in, sonny?"

If there was anything calculated to make Ted's blood boil it was being called "sonny," but he answered politely enough. "I was graduated from Forestdale High School last week."

"Oh." The auditor looked back to Carl. "Are you brothers? I heard there was a brother team working down on one of these papers."

"Heaven forbid!"

Mr. Montague turned back to Ted. "I suppose you can give me some description of the man."

Ted did, though rather inadequately, but Mr. Montague noted it all.

"Are you going to inform the police now?" asked Carl.

"I'll notify the Forestdale police, of course, now that it's known the man is operating in this territory, but I'll ask them to keep it quiet. Meanwhile, if anything more should come up, or you can think of anything else that will help us, you can reach me at my apartment." He placed his card on the desk. "I don't think it very likely that we'll catch the man, though. And if we don't, then it'll be up to the governor to decide what to do next. There may even be a special session of the Legislature. Meanwhile, I don't think it would reflect very well on your newspaper if this story should come out."

"Nor on the auditor's office, either," Carl retorted, but Mr. Montague was at the door by this time, and pretended not to hear.

"I've had something to do with Mr. Montague before," Carl explained to Ted when he had gone, "and I know the sort he is. He's one of those pompous officials who are always trying to put you in your place. Of course he has to be careful he doesn't offend anybody important. If our circulation were thirty thousand, instead of three thousand, I think he would have been just ten times as polite."

But although Carl had rushed loyally to Ted's defense while Mr. Montague was there, he was much more critical of Ted now that their visitor was gone.

"I still can't understand how you came to do such a thing, Ted. Your brain must have been turned off for a while."

"What else could I do?" Ted retorted. "He was a glib talker, had a ready explanation for everything. Wouldn't you have left the notebook when he asked you to?"

"I wouldn't have gotten myself into such a predicament in the first place. Why are you always trying to be a Helpful Hannah? It didn't have anything to do with you. He advertised for the package, let him come in and get it. If he could describe it, well and good, give it to him. Nobody could have offered a word of criticism. But giving it to him in an empty house! Honestly, Ted, do you have to have a brick fall on your head before you begin to get suspicious?"

There was no answer Ted could make to that, and so he was silent. Fundamentally, he liked to believe that all people were on the level until they had given him some reason to assume the opposite, and Mr. Denning had given him no such reason. Everything had seemed so plausible. Why, even his initials had been on the cover!

When Nelson stopped in around noon, Ted gloomily told him all about it. While Nelson didn't see how Ted could be blamed for it, he was much impressed by the fact that the state auditor himself had come to the office.

"You sure meet people in this business. Here it's only your first week, and you've already met a V.I.P."

"Better call him a V.A.I.P. That stands for Very Angry Important Person. Is this only my third day here? It seems like a century already. Just think, in only three days I've gotten not only the state auditor mad at me, but maybe the governor as well. And he even hinted at a special session of the Legislature!"

"Not many cub reporters could accomplish all that in three days," Nelson admitted with a grin. "Ron used to say the Wilfords always did everything up big. Even their blunders!"

9.

Ken Asks a Question

SOMETIME DURING the afternoon, when Ted had enough time to draw a deep breath, he decided to call the Forestdale hotel and see if any person named Denning had registered there. He didn't think it at all probable. If Mr. Denning ever had been there, he had probably registered under another name, and he would certainly be gone by now. However, it was a simple enough thing to check.

The clerk at the desk tried to be helpful. No, there had not been a Mr. Denning registered there. Furthermore, when Ted inquired about guests who had recently checked out, giving a brief description of Mr. Denning, the clerk was unable to recall anyone of that description. Ted thanked him and hung up. As he had supposed, it all came to nothing.

Certainly Ted had had his suspicions of Mr. Denning, at first when they discovered the house was empty, and later when the telephone rang. Yet, as Mr. Denning talked, his suspicions had faded away. What was it that had been most convincing? It was the initials, of course. How could you explain those initials, H.D., on the notebook?

Then, suddenly, the explanation came to Ted, so simple and yet so ludicrous that he almost laughed outright. H.D.— Harold Denning—Highway Department. Those weren't Mr.

Denning's initials; they stood simply for Highway Department!

That meant, of course, that the man's name was not Harold Denning. But still, there was the telephone number, Forestdale 8106. Ted had been at both ends of the number, on Monday afternoon when he phoned Mr. Denning from the office, and Tuesday afternoon when he received the call from Mr. Denning at the empty house. The telephone number was legitimate, and if it was legitimate, couldn't it be checked? The telephone company didn't install telephones without knowing a little bit about the subscriber. Either they made sure he was the owner of the house, or they checked his credit rating, or they made him put up a deposit or bond, or something like that. But while the telephone company might have some information about Mr. Denning, Ted didn't feel that it would do him any good to call them and inquire. They would certainly refuse to tell him, especially over the phone. The only way to get the information from them was to go down to the office with a police officer, or some other person in authority. Then perhaps they'd be willing to tell what they knew.

Ted wondered what would happen if he should dial Forestdale 8106 right now. Probably the phone was still connected, for it was unlikely Mr. Denning would have ordered it disconnected after he had recovered the plans, and equally improbable that if he had the telephone company would have filled the order so soon. Almost idly Ted dialed Forestdale 8106. He could imagine that in a moment the telephone would begin to ring, and after a dozen rings that nobody answered there would be nothing left for him to do but hang up.

However, the telephone never rang. Instead, as he finished dialing, there was a clicking on the line, and a woman's voice broke in.

"What number were you calling, please?"

"Forestdale 8106."

"I'm sorry, sir, but there is no such number."

"Oh, I'm sorry, but I called that number last Monday. I suppose it's been disconnected since."

"No, sir, that number was discontinued over two weeks ago."

"But it couldn't be," said Ted, startled. "I tell you I called it on Monday."

"I'm sorry, sir." She didn't want to argue with a customer, and she was obliged to confine herself to certain trite phrases. "Our records show that Forestdale 8106 was discontinued over two weeks ago."

"All right. Thank you," and Ted hung up.

What could it mean? Could he by accident have dialed the wrong number and by chance got Mr. Denning? No, that was so nearly impossible as to be completely unbelievable. Then he smiled. Maybe his memory had merely slipped, and the number Mr. Denning had given him wasn't Forestdale 8106 at all. He rummaged through his desk until he found the slip of paper on which he had written down the number Mr. Denning had told him. The black figures stared up at him uncompromisingly. There could be no mistake. They read Forestdale 8106.

But how could you dial a number that wasn't connected and get an answer? How could you receive a call over a disconnected telephone? As Nelson had said when they heard the telephone ringing, why was a telephone ringing in an empty house? Surely it was a ghost telephone, after all!

Ted dialed the police station. He got Sergeant Jeffers, whom he knew personally.

"I wonder, Sergeant, if you've checked yet on that empty house, where Harold Denning was supposed to have lived?"

"Yes, we did, Ted. Harold Denning wasn't the real owner,

of course. The house was sold recently, and the new owner, Mr. James Fox, is planning on moving in in a couple of weeks. We've checked on Mr. Fox, and he seems to be completely on the up and up. He was very surprised to learn that someone was using his house. He doesn't know any more about it than we do."

"Did you check on the telephone in the empty house, Sergeant?"

"Yes, we did, Ted, but it was dead."

"Dead? I received a call on it when I was out there yesterday!"

But the sergeant was a very practical man, who refused to believe in ghosts in broad daylight. "All right, Ted, if you say you received a call on it, then you did. That simply means that the phone must have been connected up yesterday and has been disconnected since."

"But I called the phone company, and they said that that phone was disconnected two weeks ago."

"Well, Ted, all I can say is that if you received a call over a phone, and the company says the phone was disconnected, either you're lying—which I don't believe—or else the phone company has made a mistake."

"They're pretty careful. They don't usually make mistakes like that. Are you sure about that number on the phone? What was it?"

The sergeant consulted his records. "It was Forestdale 8106."

"Yes, that's the number, all right," said Ted, more mystified than ever.

"Wait a minute, Ted. You say you received a call in the empty house. All right, well and good. I believe you. You claim that the number on which you received the call was Forestdale 8106. Now that's not so good. How do you know that was really the number?"

"The card on the telephone said—"

"What does that prove? Anybody could have changed the card. Maybe the phone rang, but you have no way of knowing it was the number, Forestdale 8106, that rang it. Maybe the phone was hooked up to some other number."

"But I dialed Forestdale 8106 on Monday afternoon, and I got the empty house."

"How do you know you did? You were on the other end of the line that time. Maybe Forestdale 8106 was hooked up to some other outlet miles away."

"The phone company claims it wasn't hooked up at all."

"Then the phone company must be wrong."

As Ted hung up his head was whirling. What did all this mean? Initials that weren't somebody's initials, a phone number that rang but wasn't anybody's phone number—where was all this leading? He was glad when Nelson came in, just before quitting time. Whenever Ted felt that he was soaring too far above earth, he could always count on Nelson to get his feet planted firmly on the ground again.

Ted recounted all these new developments, beginning with the initials. It took Nelson a moment to get it.

"Then if H.D. stands for Highway Department, it must have been just a coincidence that Mr. Denning had the same initials."

"Coincidence, my foot! The so-called Mr. Denning simply made up the name to account for the initials."

Then he went on to tell about the ghostlike telephone, but Nelson could offer no explanation for that, either, except to agree with Sergeant Jeffers that the phone company must have made a mistake on their records.

"But at least it proves one thing," said Nelson with a laugh. "This is no ordinary sneak thief. We're up against a pretty shrewd operator. And you've only got yourself to blame for this puzzle, Ted. Look at the simple little thing this Mr. Denning asked you to do. He just asked you to mail the notebook to him, if it should turn up. If you'd only mailed it, you never would have found out that the house was empty, you never would have learned that there was something queer about the telephone, everything would have seemed hunky-dory. The thief didn't think that the loss of the plans would be discovered for another month, and by that time he would have been so far away nobody ever would have found him. Then you came along and screwed everything up. No, you couldn't simply *mail* the notebook to him, as he asked. As Carl Allison said, you had to be a Helpful Hannah and deliver it in person. And that's where the thief's troubles began—and yours, too. Nobody could have blamed you, if you'd handled things in the ordinary way."

"I wonder, though," said Ted thoughtfully. "If I'd mailed the notebook, would the postman have delivered it to an empty house?"

"I think he would. Remember that rural box way out in front. Maybe he wouldn't even have known the house was still empty. Maybe he would have thought the new owner had moved in, or was just about to move in. He would have put the package in the box. Of course, if it was still there after a few days, he probably would have reclaimed it and begun to ask questions about it. But that wouldn't have happened. Mr. Denning would have had his big, fat mitts on it before that."

"Still, I wonder if he wasn't taking a chance on that mailing business? Why didn't he simply come down to the office in person every few days, to see if the parcel had been turned in?"

"No, Ted, I don't think so. Maybe he took a chance on the mailing, because something might go wrong, but a thief has to take chances, and it didn't look to him like as big a chance as the other way. Remember, he thought the theft wouldn't be discovered for a month, but he couldn't be *sure* about it. His best bet was not to come to this office any more than he absolutely had to. He had to come once, to pay for the ad and help quiet any suspicions you might have had, but no, sir, he wasn't going to come back if he could get out of it. He hoped you'd simply mail the package to him, and solve all his problems. What if the theft had been discovered? Or what if the finder had broken the lock open, so that it was known what the package contained? He wanted to stay as far out of the reach of the police as it was possible for him to get."

"Well, he got the plans away from me, and I'm not very proud of the way he did it. But what can I do about it now?"

"That's easy," said Nelson blithely. "All you've got to do is capture Mr. Denning and recover the plans. You've got a big scoop waiting for you, if you'll just go after it."

"Go after it? The way work's piling up, I'm lucky if I can break away from the office for ten minutes. Anyway, what can I do to catch Mr. Denning that the police aren't doing?"

"Nothing, I guess," Nelson agreed mournfully.

That evening at home Ted got a call from Ken Kutler.

"Ted? Ken here. I'd like to talk to you about this highway-plans business. Can I come over?"

It always exasperated Ted to learn that his rival had caught on to a story that was supposed to be secret, but he had to admire the way Ken usually managed it.

"Sure, Ken, come on."

Ted was sitting on the glider on the front porch reading the newspaper when Ken drove up. Folding up the paper, Ted stepped down to the curb. Ken got out of the car, and it being a warm, pleasant evening, they stood outside talking, leaning against the car.

"I thought it was a secret story, Ken, but you seem to be on it almost as soon as I was."

"It was reported to the police this morning, and so of course I picked it up soon after."

"Wasn't this supposed to be confidential?"

"Well, I had to make certain promises in order to get the information. I didn't like it, but that's the way it had to be."

"Exactly what did you promise?" Ted inquired.

"I promised that I wouldn't print any story that might jeopardize the recovery of the plans, and that's all I would promise. Mr. Montague would like more than that. He'd like me to promise that I'd sit on this story forever, but I couldn't go for that. Too much hush-hush on political matters leads straight down the road to corruption. After all, pompous and self-righteous as he tries to appear, his own hands aren't any too clean on this matter, and I'm not covering up for any politician's mistakes."

He asked for further details of the affair, and Ted told him everything he knew. When he came to the story of the initials, Ken had to laugh at Ted's disgusted expression, and Ted joined in. After Ted had told how he left the notebook in the empty house, he asked:

"Would you have done that, Ken?"

"No, Ted, I don't believe I would, but don't go by me. I've got an uncomfortably suspicious nature. Persons like yourself who believe this is a pretty good, upright, honest world are as refreshing as a summer breeze. I'm sure I wouldn't have left a possibly valuable package in an empty house, and I doubt that I would have tried to deliver it in person at all. And if Mr. Denning had come into my office and asked for the package, I would have asked him to describe the contents and then would have opened it to check. Simply describing a lost article on the *outside* isn't always enough to establish ownership. But heck, maybe I'm only second guessing. If he'd come upon me in a busy moment, I might have simply handed the parcel to him and said, 'Take it and be gone.' "

"Would you have mailed it to him, as he asked?"

"That's something different again, Ted. Yes, I believe I would have mailed it to him. That was a perfectly legitimate request. Lots of people are busy and just don't have time to go running around on errands like that. But if I were a prudent person, I believe I would have telephoned him once more before I mailed it. Unfortunately, I'm not always so careful as I ought to be."

They continued to discuss the case for some time afterward, but in the final analysis, as Ken prepared to leave, Ted was disappointed. Ken was a shrewd person, and Ted, who valued his judgments, had been hoping right along that Ken would come out with some new idea that would help throw light on the series of strange events. However, he offered nothing. The problem of the mysterious telephone puzzled him just as much as it did Ted and the others. But that Ken was beginning to get a hunch of some sort was plain to Ted, for he had known Ken for a long time and had had a chance to observe his mind at work. On the other hand, he knew just as certainly that Ken wouldn't tell him what it was until he had had some chance to put his theory to the test. At last Ken said:

"Ted, I've got a queer little bug in my bonnet. I can't prove it, so I'm not going to tell you what it is. But you've been so considerate to me that I owe it to you to give you any help I can. I'll put it in the form of a question. I don't expect an answer, and I'm not going to answer any further questions about it myself. It's simply this:

"Are you sure that the thing you're looking for is really the highway plans?"

10.

A Message from a Haunted House

WHAT DID it all mean? Apparently Mr. Denning had stolen the new highway plans, accidentally lost them, and Ted had returned them, acting on instructions over a telephone that wasn't even connected. Now Ken had suggested they weren't really the highway plans. Then what was Mr. Denning doing, and why was Mr. Montague so upset? The state auditor had now reported the theft to the police, and surely he wouldn't have done that if the plans weren't missing, would he? But Ted had known Ken too long and too well to dismiss lightly anything he said. Even if Ted wasn't able to fathom Ken's meaning, it was something he ought to keep in mind for future reference.

And that error Mr. White appeared to have made, concerning the time when Mr. Denning called him. Ted was beginning to believe now that Mr. White *hadn't* been mistaken. Why would Mr. Denning call the office *after* talking with Ted? Because he wanted it to appear that he had talked to the office first to explain how he knew Ted was out at the empty house. He had probably tried to get the office immediately after talking with Ted, but unfortunately for him Mr. White was a little late getting back to the office, and it was ten minutes later before he could reach him. That ten minutes had served to arouse Ted's suspicions. But how had Mr. Denning known Ted was out at the empty house, if he hadn't called the office first?

Ted remembered, too, that Mr. Denning wasn't the first person who had been interested in the new highway and later disappeared. There was also Mr. Gray, who had pretended to have a missing dog. It seemed that whenever big profits were in sight, a lot of unscrupulous characters were attracted like—to use Ron's favorite expression—fleas to a hound.

However, Ted was forced to push these speculations to the back of his mind, for Thursday morning proved his busiest time to date. There was the Thursday-noon deadline creeping up on him, faster than he had anticipated. True, he had gone through nearly the same thing on Monday morning, but the difference was that then Miss Monroe had had everything blocked out for him. This time he was on his own.

The remaining stories—not a great many—which had not yet been set up in type had to go to the printer, and many other stories had to be proofread and corrected, and fitted into the dummy. One of these stories Ted had not seen before. It had been written by Carl, who had typed it and turned it in to the printer himself.

As Ted read Carl's story, he began to frown. It was written in Carl's careful way, and yet—something about it seemed wrong. Ted read it over again, and still couldn't figure out what was the matter. He read it a third time—and suddenly it leaped out at him. Great day, could it be true? For the next few minutes he became very busy on the telephone, and then leaned back in his chair with a sigh. Carl had made that mistake which newspapermen recognize as so dangerous— he had confused two different persons who happened to have the same name. There was no help for it, the story would have to come out of the paper. Ted knew that he ought to consult Carl about it first, but Carl was out of town on an assignment for the day and couldn't be reached.

But a blank column on the front page. What could he use to fill it at this late date? Ted was almost frantic. There were plenty of lesser stories he could have used, but he hadn't followed them up because he hadn't expected to have extra space. Now he had the space and no stories, and it was too late to do anything about them.

He thought of the stack of mail—that secondary pile of material that could be used or not as the occasion warranted. He knew he wouldn't find anything very important there, for all the important items had already been pulled out. Still, he might be able to find something good enough for a column. As a matter of fact, he had no other choice.

He ran a sheet of paper into his typewriter, then began to go through the mail. It consisted mostly of press-agent releases on personalities or products. Whenever he came to an item he could use, he wrote it down. When he thought he had enough to fill a column, he ran the last sheet out of his typewriter and took them all to the printer, feeling rather uncomfortable about the incident. While it was true that Mr. Dobson occasionally used material of this kind, he never used a whole column of it at one time—nor did he place it in the first column of the first page, the second most prominent location in the paper. But Ted couldn't help that now—it was too late to remake the page.

Sometime that morning—just one of a number of telephone calls—Sergeant Jeffers phoned.

"Ted, I've checked with the phone company about that call you received out at the empty house. They can't explain it. You and I had more or less concluded that they must have made a mistake about when the phone was disconnected, but they claim they didn't. In fact, they're getting rather testy about the way I've been insisting they are wrong. And I must admit all I've got to go on is that you tell me you received a call on that telephone Tuesday afternoon."

"I received it, all right. My friend Nelson Morgan heard it, too. How can it be explained?"

"I don't know, Ted. The only thing I could think of was a mistake at the phone company, which they deny." His voice sounded hesitant. "Of course even big utilities are run by human beings, just like the rest of us, and nobody likes admitting he's made a mistake. But they have one strong point in their favor. They say that at the time the phone was disconnected the lineman noticed that the cable was rather frayed, so he took it down. Then, for some reason or other, he didn't replace it at once. At the time you claim you received the call, Ted, there wasn't even any connection between the house and the telephone pole!"

"Do you think I'm lying?" asked Ted evenly.

"Of course not. I'm just wondering if maybe you've made a mistake."

"What kind of mistake?"

"Well, are you sure you were in *this* empty house?"

"Are there any other empty houses on the same road?"

"No, we've checked that. And you say the number card on the telephone read Forestdale 8106. That all jibes. I'm just wondering, Ted—are you sure you're not trying to pull off a practical joke this time?"

"I'm perfectly sure. I've got my hands too full just now to worry about that sort of thing, thank you!"

"That's what I thought, Ted. Don't get huffy about it—I was just asking. But I'm hanged if I can see any other explanation for it. You're sure that call didn't come from anywhere within the house?"

"Yes, I'm sure of that. We looked."

Further speculation seemed to be useless, and the officer

hung up. Ted returned to his work. He was interrupted again toward the end of the morning by the arrival of a visitor. Although he was anxious to put the finishing touches on the paper, he realized he had to be polite. Outsiders had no way of realizing which were the busiest times for the staff.

"What can I do for you?" asked Ted, swinging around in the swivel chair.

"My name is Sterling Lamont, and I'm from the Highway Department."

Ted's eyes narrowed. He had had so many odd experiences lately that he found himself less willing to accept anyone on faith. "Do you have any identification, Mr. Lamont?"

The man smiled. "Oh, yes. Here." He took out his wallet and showed an identification card. It looked authentic enough, but still, a card like that could be forged fairly easily. Noticing Ted's hesitation, the man went on, "My car's just out in front."

Glancing out through the large plate-glass window, Ted saw an official car, with the name of the department painted in gold letters. A car could be stolen, too—but hang it, how suspicious could you get? Anyway, Mr. Lamont soon showed from his knowledge of the case that he was exactly what he claimed to be.

"Please sit down, Mr. Lamont. I take it you're working under Mr. Montague?"

"Oh, no," said Mr. Lamont, accepting his invitation. "Mr. Montague is in auditing, and I'm in highways, but naturally we're just as interested in learning what happened to the plans and doing anything we can to help recover them. Did Mr. Montague say anything to you about the importance of getting the plans back?"

"Yes, he seemed to believe that the thief might find them very profitable if he were interested in speculating."

"Well, yes, that's true enough. However, I don't think that's the thing that has Mr. Montague so agitated. He's worried about how this is going to reflect upon his department when the news comes out. Mr. Montague is rather— But then, I don't have to tell you anything about him. You've met him already."

Ted nodded.

"I don't know, Ted, that there is anything you can do to help me, but I thought it best to keep in touch with you just in case anything should turn up. The police have been notified, I suppose?"

"The Forestdale police, yes, and I think Mr. Montague also has some private sources at work on the theft. He didn't want to talk about that."

"Oh, yes, that's typical of Mr. Montague. He's been rather close-lipped about the theft, even with us, which is the reason I may not be perfectly informed on all the details. I know, in a general way, how you recovered the plans and then by a ruse were led to turn them over to the thief. There is only one way I can think of you might help. Would you be able to recognize Mr. Denning's voice if you heard it again?"

"Maybe not just his voice. But I would know him if I saw him again."

"You saw him? He came to this office?" Mr. Lamont seemed rather taken aback. "I didn't know that. This puts rather a different complexion on the affair. It may turn out that you are a very important witness, Ted, and perhaps our only witness."

"That's so," Ted agreed. "I didn't think of that before."

The man rose to his feet. "Well, I won't take up any more of your time, Ted. I can see how busy you are. I understand your editor has been hospitalized following an accident. How's he getting on?"

"Oh, pretty well. I hear he's been allowed a few visitors."

"That's good. I imagine it must be some satisfaction to him to know he's left the paper in such good hands." Mr. Lamont was smiling, but Ted always retained a healthy skepticism toward flattery.

Seeing that he hadn't made as good an impression as he expected, Mr. Lamont did not pursue the subject. "Well, Ted, I just wanted to say that if anything should turn up, anything at all, that you think might help me, I'd be awfully glad to have you call me at the Highway Department's central office. You've been put to a good deal of trouble so far, but I suppose it will be worth it if you get a good story out of it."

"I'm afraid I don't see a story in it so far," Ted responded.

Mr. Lamont caught his meaning more readily than Ted had expected. "You mean Mr. Montague has asked you to kill it?"

"Well—just to hold it back until he gives permission."

"And if I know Mr. Montague as well as I think I do, you'll never get that permission—not even when it's too late to matter any more. He won't be anxious to be shown up in print." He smiled again, said, "Well, good-by, and thanks, Ted," and left.

In spite of the interruptions, Ted managed to put the paper to bed on time, and went out to lunch. On his way back, he passed near the hospital, and decided to stop in for a minute. After all, if Mr. Dobson had been allowed some visitors, wouldn't he want to see Ted? But when the clerk at the desk saw him, she looked doubtful.

"I think you'd better get permission from Dr. Pearson first, Ted."

"But Mr. Dobson's had visitors, hasn't he?"

"Well, yes, but— I believe that's Dr. Pearson coming in now. You can ask him."

Approaching the doctor, Ted was about to frame his request when he noticed the doctor shaking his head, even before Ted had started to speak.

"Sorry, Ted, nothing doing."

"But why can't I see him?" Ted argued. "Other people go in."

"If you could go in as a friend, Ted, that would be all well and good. But the minute you step through that door you'll be bringing all the troubles of the newspaper with you."

"I'd try not to talk about the newspaper, if you don't want me to."

"Sorry, Ted, but Mr. Dobson wouldn't let you. He'd be inquiring into every detail, and before I knew what was coming off he'd be trying to run the newspaper from his hospital bed."

"Wouldn't it relieve his mind a little to know just how we're getting on?"

"He knows that already, Ted. He can read the finished paper when it comes out. That's as much as I want him to do for now."

"Well, then, when can I see him? There are a few things that have come up that I think he ought to know about."

"It'll be at least a week before I'll want you in that room, Ted, and maybe longer. To put it bluntly, you're the very last person I want him to see. I know it isn't easy for you trying to run the paper like this, but you'll just have to handle things in the way that seems best to you. I've seen enough of you in the past to know that you usually manage to carry on pretty well."

Coming from an old friend like Dr. Pearson, this did not seem like flattery, and Ted returned to the office feeling somewhat happier. That afternoon, although there was still plenty to do, he no longer felt that time was breathing hotly down his neck. He could now give his attention to planning the next issue, and he had time to think and plan without being under too much pressure. He went to work drawing up the new dummy. He knew which big advertisers had already renewed, and he could allot their space. There were also the allotments for the regular features, and he had tentatively decided where to place a few of the stories. He couldn't do much more than that until he was sure about the rest of the advertisers, so he turned his attention to the mail.

Late in the afternoon Nelson came in, and Ted acquainted him with all the latest details.

"Well, what do you want to do now?" asked Nelson.

"I sort of think I'd like to take a ride out to the empty house again. Maybe there's something on the scene there that we've overlooked."

"O.K. by me, only I thought you were so busy."

"Oh, things have simmered down a little, now that my deadline's past."

He went over to the back door of the office and opened it. The presses were busily humming. "I'm leaving now, Mr. White. Don't bother answering the phone. If it's anything important they can call back," for Ted knew that this was the busiest time for the printing department.

"O.K., Ted."

Out at the empty house they were fortunate, for a telephone lineman was just descending from the pole nearest to the empty house. He was a young man, and apparently had no objection to talking to them as he rolled up his wires and began putting his tools away.

"Are you sure the telephone in this house wasn't connected last Tuesday?" Ted inquired.

"I sure am. I took this cable down myself two weeks ago, and I've just finished putting it back up."

"Could anyone have put up a temporary cable in the meantime?"

The repairman considered. "I don't think so. I think I would have noticed if anybody'd been tampering with my work up on the pole."

"Then how come the telephone was ringing last Tuesday?" Nelson demanded.

"Let me explain this to you," said the man good-naturedly. "You see these wires? Electricity flows through them. There's two lines in each cable, so the electricity can go both ways. Somebody at the other end of the line talks into a telephone, which disturbs the current, and when the current gets to you it disturbs your telephone, and you can hear. No wires, no telephone, and that's that."

"What about ship-to-shore telephones?" asked Ted. "They talk, and there aren't any wires."

"That's something different. The current goes out over radio waves, and you have to get a permit from the federal government to use your particular band of radio waves. The same is true of car telephones. And let me tell you something: just try using a band without official permission, and you'll find yourself in trouble so fast it'll make your head swim. Ask any ham operator who's accidentally slipped off his proper frequency. All channels are constantly monitored."

"What about walkie-talkies?" Nelson inquired.

"Same thing. You still need official permission."

"But their range is so small," Ted pointed out, "only about a mile, I've heard. Could someone have hooked up a walkie-talkie so that it would work on the telephone in this house, and hoped that because of the short range he might not get caught?"

"It would be a pretty difficult technical problem to operate a telephone from a walkie-talkie, and the current is so weak I'm pretty sure it wouldn't ring a bell."

"Couldn't you step it up?"

"I think it would still be pretty hard, and require a lot of extra equipment. Until I saw it done, I would question that you could fool anybody into thinking it was a regular telephone call."

That seemed to be that, but Ted had one more question.

"Is it your general practice to leave a telephone in an empty house after it's been disconnected? Don't you take the telephone out, too?"

"Not always. That's pretty much up to the lineman. If he thought the telephone was going to be reconnected soon, and wasn't likely to be damaged in the meantime, he might just leave it there. That's what I did this time."

After the telephone man drove off, they strolled up toward the house.

"You know something?" Nelson observed. "I think he's right about that wire. Look how low it hangs, reaching from the pole to the house. If it had been there before, I think we would have noticed it—especially after that call came through."

"You could be right," Ted half agreed.

They did not go into the house, but wandered around to the rear. Everything seemed very isolated and deserted. There was a gardener's cottage, also empty, a tool shed, and a small greenhouse. The neat lawn and well-planned garden descended on easy terraces down to a small ravine and a brook. Beyond that were woods. No other houses were in sight. They saw nothing further of interest, and returned slowly to the car.

After supper, when his mother had gone out to a club meeting, Ted finally got around to looking at his mail before turning to the evening paper and the work he had brought home from the office. One letter puzzled him. The name and address were printed, and there was no return address. He opened it and read:

"If you want to know something more about the missing plans, come to Everett House tonight at nine o'clock. Bring a friend, if you like, but *no police*. An Acquaintance."

Everett House? That was an abandoned house way out on the other side of the ridge, Ted recalled. He didn't know much about it other than that it was said to be haunted. But haunted or not, it was at least another empty house, like the first empty house that had led to all his present troubles.

11.

A Predicament

IF HE WERE going out to Everett House that night, he would have to ask Nelson to take him. Nelson's car, such as it was, was a prerequisite for the trip. Although Ted still tried to reason himself out of it, he had known from the first moment he read the note that he was going somehow. He had convinced himself that he was in no personal danger, and Mr. Lamont's remarks about his being the only witness had not changed his opinion. Besides, even if there was an element of personal danger, he decided to go anyway. The adventure of it—a call from an unknown person to come to a reputedly haunted house at the hour of twilight—intrigued him, but although this was his most important motive, he tried to convince himself there was something more. Having returned the missing plans to the thief, Ted felt it was his duty to do anything he could which might help get them back. And the writer of the anonymous note must know something about the plans. If not, why would he write to Ted at all?

But endangering himself and endangering a friend who had no personal involvement in the situation were two entirely different things, and Ted hesitated before calling Nelson. If he called, he knew Nelson would go along with him, so the responsibility lay on his shoulders. After weighing everything carefully, he decided to call.

"All right. When do we start?" was Nelson's response, as soon as Ted had explained the matter to him.

"You're sure you want to go? I'm not exactly convinced it's dangerous, but still—"

"Oh, what have I got to live for, anyway? Just college ahead, and I'll probably flunk out the first semester, and be sent home in disgrace. Might as well die now while I'm still ahead of the game."

"If you'll stop babbling a minute, we'll figure out what we'd better do. Think we'd better tell anybody where we're going?"

"Don't see how I can, Ted, unless you want me to spill the whole story of the missing plans. I'll just say I'm going somewhere with you, and not to worry if I'm late getting back. But you can explain it to your mother if you want to. She knows more about the plans."

"I don't have that problem now. My mother's out for the evening, so I'll just leave her a note. I can't mention Everett House, though, or she'd worry."

"Too bad. Then they'll never know where to look for the bodies."

Nelson agreed to come over directly, and as he waited Ted wrote a hurried note for his mother. He said that he'd been called out of town on an errand for the paper and might be very late getting back. Acting on a hunch, he added that if he found it was going to be too late, he would stop over for the night. Leaving the note where his mother would be sure to find it, he hurried outside as Nelson's car pulled up.

"Tell me all about Everett House," Nelson requested as they headed out on the open road. "I want to be good and scared before I get there."

"Well, all this happened back when I was a little kid, so all I know is what I've been told. It seems that Mr. Everett lived out there alone with his wife. Not very much was known about either of them, and where facts are lacking, fiction begins. A good many stories were spread about Mr. Everett's sinister background, but as far as I know nothing was ever proved.

"Anyway, the couple kept pretty much to themselves. There were no close neighbors, and apparently they didn't want to have anything to do with the neighbors they did have. Nobody could figure out why they'd want to live all alone out there, anyway. It was just a ramshackle old house which hadn't been kept up. There were never any electric lights on the place, and it isn't even certain there was any water—at least toward the end.

"This was how things stood until one day a neighbor driving past noticed the front door standing ajar. He thought that looked very strange, and he went to investigate. He found the house empty. Apparently all the furniture had been moved out during the night, and judging by the tracks following a recent rainfall, it must have been just the night before.

"The neighbor called the sheriff, and the sheriff came to look the place over. He had his dog with him, and it's said that the dog, instead of following them to the house, dashed off until he came to the well. There he crouched down and bristled, acting both fierce and afraid. The men came after him, and discovered that the well had caved in. Nobody knew when it had happened, but it was hard to understand how the couple had been able to live there very long without water.

"Then they tried to get the dog to come into the house with them, but he simply lay down and refused to budge. It was impossible to get him to come anywhere near the house, except by dragging him. Well, the men went inside but failed to discover anything, except for a few spots which might have meant anything.

"Nothing was ever heard of either Mr. Everett or his wife after that. But persons driving past after dark have claimed to hear strange noises and to see flashing lights."

"Who owns Everett House now?"

"The county, I guess. It must have gone for taxes long ago. And nobody wants to buy it, even at a cut-rate tax sale. It just isn't worth fixing up, and then, with no lights and no water, it isn't much of a bargain. Anyway, that's the excuse that's given. Maybe the real reason is that people are afraid of the ghost that's supposed to be inhabiting the place."

"Whose ghost?"

"Mrs. Everett's, I suppose. Nobody says so, but the implication is that her husband murdered her, buried her in the well, and then disappeared."

"Would he have taken the furniture with him?"

"Must have. Where else did it go?"

"Some story." Nelson grinned. "I don't mind going there just for a visit, as they say, but I don't think I'd want the place even if they gave it to me. I hope your letter writer is on time. Twilight is all right, but I'd just as soon not hang around after dark. Say, wasn't it funny how he signed his letter? Most letters like that are signed A Friend."

"Probably he isn't lying about that. He must be an acquaintance, but he doesn't claim to be a friend. Let's just hope he doesn't turn out to be an enemy."

Their route led around the ridge of hills that lay to the west of Forestdale and along the opposite slopes. As the road rose into the hills, the scene became ever wilder and more desolate. Few cars were passed, and finally none at all. Only occasionally did they glimpse small homesteads set well back from the road. Paving had long since given way to gravel, and soon the gravel was replaced by a plain dirt road.

"This would be a heck of a place to get stuck in the mud," Nelson observed, "and by the looks of things we may be having some rain before morning."

"I wasn't planning on staying all night," Ted rejoined.

"No, but navigating through here in the dark would be no picnic, either. You know something, though, it would be kind of a thrill to spend a night in a haunted house, wouldn't it? It would sure give us something to talk about, especially at the senior picnic."

"Remember that 'Wandering Reporter' column we ran in the school newspaper? We once asked the question, 'Would you be willing to spend a night alone in a haunted house?' None of the girls would do it, but about half the boys said they wouldn't mind, as long as they weren't breaking any law. One guy got pretty high-toned, said there wasn't anything to be afraid of except your own imagination."

"And, boy, that can sometimes be the most frightening thing of all," Nelson retorted.

Although they had never been to Everett House before, they knew the way, and there were so few intersections that there was little chance of going astray. The sun had set, and an ever-deepening twilight shadowed the fields as they ascended the last hill which would take them to their destination.

Near the top of the hill a drive ran off from the main road, leading to Everett House. Nelson turned up the drive, then drew to a stop. The drive was too rutty and overgrown with tall weeds to allow passage for the car without a great deal of trouble. They could just see the roof peak of Everett House beyond, over another slight rise.

This was a wilderness in summer, with birds nesting, wild flowers brilliant with color, the constant humming of insect life. Once this might have been a prosperous farm, but all signs of human habitation were gradually disappearing. At least half the fence was down, in places the drive itself was indistinguishable, and as they approached the house they found that this, too, was slowly going to pieces. Shutters hung down on broken hinges, several panes of glass were missing, the house itself looked as though it had never known a coat of paint.

"I've wondered how any house could stay empty so long in these days of the housing shortage," Ted remarked, "but this is no house. It's a—"

"A hangout for haunts," Nelson concluded. "Sure glad I brought a flashlight along. It must be almost pitch black inside."

"Don't see any sign of anyone around," Ted observed. "Want to go in?"

"Guess we'll have to. I imagine this other party has his eye on us, and isn't going to show up till he's sure we're all right. Well, let's go. What are you waiting for, cold feet?"

"No colder than yours, I'll bet, but take it easy and watch your step. There may be some boards missing from the floor."

The door pushed open on squeaky hinges. Flashing the light before them, they advanced into the house. The floor, though well worn, looked substantial enough and did nothing more than give off a few ominous creaks as they moved forward with tentative steps. At last they stood in the middle of the room, and Nelson flashed the light around them. The wallpaper was faded and loose in spots from moisture. There were no lighting fixtures so the former occupants must have depended on lamps.

This was an empty house only in the sense that it was unoccupied and nothing of value remained, but it had not been cleaned out as had the other empty house they had visited. That house had been awaiting new occupants; this one looked as though it would never be occupied again. There were pieces of broken furniture around, not worth moving, many old boxes, and even a stack of old newspapers that had been gnawed into shreds by mice or squirrels.

"I visited a museum once," Nelson remarked, "and it gave me the same creepy feeling. Oh, it was clean enough, but dark and gloomy, and with a lot of remnants of dead things around. They even had skeletons."

"Don't be too sure there aren't any around here. You could try looking in some of those old trunks."

"No, thank you, my friend. Even if we didn't find a skeleton, we'd be likely to uncover some of your rat friends."

"I didn't say they were my friends. I just thought we ought to get to know each other better."

It was still a few minutes before nine o'clock, and there was nothing much they could do except pull up some old boxes and sit down and wait until such time as "An Acquaintance" chose to show himself. A thick layer of dust covered everything. It rose in a faint cloud whenever they touched anything; even their footprints were visible on the floor. Over by the windows, on the lighter side of the house, they could see numerous cobwebs. Flies were buzzing about, but their minutes were numbered, for it wouldn't be long before their wings became entangled in some of those silvery threads.

"We're likely to end up with silicosis or pneumonia, breathing in all this dust," Nelson complained. "Then everybody'll be sorry."

"Who?"

"I don't know, but there ought to be *somebody* who'll be sorry."

But if they avoided the highly improbable complication of silicosis, and didn't allow themselves to get scared to death, what else did the night hold for them? Although Ted didn't mention it, Mr. Lamont's words came back to him, and it occurred to him that it wasn't a very smart thing for the only witness in an important case to be sitting in a desolate house with night fast approaching.

The minutes ticked slowly by. At ten after nine their host still had not shown himself. They were beginning to grow restless as nine-fifteen came and went.

"I don't like this," Nelson whispered. "It's beginning to look like he's never coming. How long are we going to wait?"

"Till nine-thirty, and not one minute past," said Ted firmly.

"You'd think he'd be almost certain to get here in plenty of time—or even earlier so he could look us over. We'll play along for another fifteen minutes, and then that's it. If he's got anything to tell us, he'll have to contact us in a different way."

"Do you really think he has some information for us?" asked Nelson.

"Oh, I'm sure he's got some information, but whether or not he ever had any intention of giving it to us is another question. It's beginning to look like he didn't."

"Then what are we doing out here anyway? Is this just a joke?"

"I wouldn't know, but it doesn't look like it to me. It couldn't be some of our friends playing a joke on us, because they don't know enough about the case. And if it's got anything to do with those road plans, chances are it's deadly serious."

By nine-thirty it had grown so dark inside they could barely see each other. Outside, only the faintest remnant of daylight remained, and that was fading fast as more and more stars appeared in the sky. Even these were fewer than they might have been, for clouds were gathering, too, and rain could not be many hours away.

At exactly nine-thirty Ted snapped to his feet. "All right, this is it. Let's go."

In silence Nelson followed him to the door. They went outside, down the drive, to the place where their car was parked. Rather, it was the place where their car *had* been parked, for now no sign of it remained.

"Well, what do you know?" Nelson exclaimed in surprise. "You don't think that was the whole purpose of this trip, just to steal my heap, do you?"

"No, I don't think so," said Ted grimly. "What's your car worth, anyway?"

"Well, I paid only three hundred for it, but I wouldn't have taken a thousand for it—because that would be stealing. But I didn't hear the motor, did you?"

"No, and you'd think we would, because you don't have the quietest engine in the county."

Since his car was insured, Nelson was not taking his loss too seriously. It was their present predicament that interested him now.

"Well, what do we do now? Hoof it?"

"Hoof it to where? We're about fifteen miles this side of nowhere. We have a big choice of trying to find our way in the dark, sleeping out in the open in the rain, or going back to the haunted house. Which will it be?"

"Oh, the haunted house, by all means. Even if I don't live through the night, it will make an interesting story for my grandchildren to hear."

It was hardly necessary to point out to Nelson that if he didn't last the night there weren't going to be any grandchildren to hear of his exploits. However, the idea of a haunted house was not too unattractive to them. Spending a night like that is something that is often discussed but seldom done. Perhaps they could become heroes in a minor way, and Ted could even envision a feature story about it for the *Town Crier*.

Nelson's flashlight guided them back to the house, and they went inside. Nothing had changed or been disturbed, but their experience was too limited for them to know whether this was normal for a haunted house.

"Anyway, we're not in any danger until midnight," said Nelson, stretching. "That's when the spooks are supposed to walk."

The evening being slightly cool, they had worn jackets, which they now took off and folded up to make pillows for themselves. Then they cleared a place in the middle of the floor, and lay down to rest if they could.

"Just the same, I'd like it just as well if none of your rat friends decide to run over me in the night," Nelson declared.

"Why worry about the rats? They'd be more scared than you are."

"Sure, they'd be scared, but they'd be *whole*. I might be scared with a piece out of me."

They were not especially hungry, although their usual evening snack was missing, but they knew they would be by breakfast time.

"We'll get an early start out of here, as soon as day breaks," Ted decided. "We've got a long way to go, and I don't know how the transportation will be. I've got a full day coming up at the office and don't want to be late. Besides, your mother may be worrying, even if mine isn't."

"Oh, my mother never worries when I'm out with you. I guess she doesn't know you very well."

They talked for a while, but at last their voices trailed off. The person who had stolen the car was probably miles away by now, and how could an empty house hurt them? The walls didn't have arms to grasp them, the darkness couldn't smother them, the random articles scattered about had no power to move by their own volition. Sleep gradually began to overtake them.

Then the telephone rang, loud and insistently.

12.

Some Noisy Spooks

"CATALINA CATFISH!" Nelson exclaimed. "What's a tele-phone doing in a dump like this? The telephone company would never leave a phone connected up in an abandoned house."

Ted was already on his feet. "Let's try to find the telephone, and then maybe we'll have the answer," he said practically.

The bell, which continued to ring loudly, seemed to be coming from somewhere in the next room. With the aid of the flashlight, they made their way to it. Nelson flashed the beam about. The ringing now sounded as though it was coming from behind a pile of junk in the corner of the room. They found the instrument with little trouble, and Ted answered.

"Hello."

"Ted?"

"Who is this calling?"

"Never mind who this is. I'll do the talking and you listen until I ask a question. Then I want an answer, and I want it fast. It's about those highway plans. Is your paper printing them?"

"We haven't so far," said Ted, trying to sound cool.

"I know that. Are you going to?"

"I really couldn't say." In spite of the eerie atmosphere, Ted was feeling less frightened than he had expected. It's easy enough to make threats over a telephone. As a newspaperman had once pointed out, if a person refuses to give his name it's probably because he's afraid, and you don't have to worry about threats from a person like that.

"Don't get smart with me, young man. I know Mr. Dobson's sick. In his absence, who is it that decides whether the plans get printed?"

"I suppose *I* have as much to say about it as anyone," Ted answered boldly. Apparently this man didn't know the plans were gone and Ted couldn't have published them even if he wanted to. Ted resolved not to let him know.

"All right, Ted, now listen carefully because I'm going to say it only once. I want to make sure that you don't print those plans in the paper, see? Not *one word*, do you get that? And don't think I don't mean business, because I do. I brought you up there just to show you that I meant it, so don't try to doublecross me."

The man hung up. More puzzled than frightened, Ted did the same.

"Who was it? What did he say?" asked Nelson impatiently.

"His voice was sort of muffled. I didn't recognize it."

"You think it was somebody you know?"

"Maybe not. It might be somebody who was afraid I might recognize his voice *in the future*. Anyway, he doesn't want me to publish the plans. He must have known I had the plans but doesn't know I no longer have them."

"Why didn't you let him think you *were* going to publish the plans, Ted? It would have been interesting to see what he would do next. It might have brought everything to a head."

"Sure, *my* head," Ted responded. "It happened so fast I didn't have a chance to think about it. I don't know, though. I don't care much about putting up a bluff. The trouble is I can't be sure how much he knows, and if I try to bluff I might give myself away without realizing it. He isn't telling me everything he knows, and so I think the best thing I can do is not to let him know how much *I* know."

"Especially since you don't know much," Nelson kidded. "It looks like we came out here for nothing. That's a funny telephone, isn't it? Old-fashioned. I've never seen one like it, except in old movies."

"Yes, it looks like it's been here as long as the house. But even old-fashioned telephones had to have wires. I didn't notice any wires when we came in. My guess, subject to correction in the morning, is that there isn't a telephone pole within a mile of here."

"Say," said Nelson in an awed voice, "you don't suppose there's anybody in the house here with us, do you?"

"I don't know, but let's look."

"You don't think we're in any danger, do you?"

"It doesn't strike me that way. It sounded as though he didn't intend to do anything to me unless I published those plans."

The search did not take long, for the house was not a large one. There was no attic and no basement, several cubbyholes taking the place of the former, and a crawl space beneath the house substituting for the latter. After searching the interior, and feeling certain there was no one else in the house with them, they went outside. Nelson flashed his light under the house, but there was no one there, nor did it seem likely that a man could have been hidden under there earlier. If he had, it was hardly likely he could have managed to squeeze out without their having heard him.

"Well, I guess that's it," said Ted dully. "A telephone rings in an empty house, yet there's no one else in the house, and no wires leading away from the house. How do you figure that?"

"It's a ghost, for sure. Is it midnight yet?"

"Not yet. Over half an hour to go."

"Well, this ghost walks early, then, or do you suppose he could be on daylight-saving time?"

"I don't know how they work those things in ghostland. If you ever find out, let me know."

There was nothing else to do except return to the empty house and see if they could manage a little sleep. They lay down again, but they were more wakeful than before. They became aware of the great stillness about them, and the things which came along from time to time to disturb that stillness. An owl hooted, a frog boomed out, soon there was the low rumble of distant thunder.

At one point, as Ted was about to fall asleep, Nelson suddenly grabbed his arm and exclaimed:

"What's that?"

"What's what?" asked Ted sleepily.

"That noise. It sounds like footsteps. Listen."

They listened, and something came to them which did sound very much like footsteps.

"Shades of Hamlet's ghost! It's Mrs. Everett!"

Then the noise changed into a quick scamper of small feet, and they knew that whatever it was wasn't human.

"Some animal on the roof," Ted decided. "Squirrel maybe, or a rat, or maybe a bird. Nothing that could call up over a telephone, I'm sure of that."

"Especially a telephone without wires," Nelson murmured, with assumed fearfulness.

Nelson was not timid, and Ted was sure that he was enjoying himself hugely. On the other hand, the circumstances under which they found themselves were very strange. It may have been that even Nelson was more alarmed than he wanted to appear, and tried to cover it up by acting very frightened. Ted himself was not feeling particularly calm and easy about the way things were going. With so many strange things going on that couldn't be explained, who could tell what their purpose was, and where it was going to lead? His own responsibilities on the paper were already severe enough, and he wished that he had an older, more experienced hand to guide him. But that was out of the question, until Mr. Dobson was better.

There were other strange noises during the night, squeaking boards, flapping of shutters, even the rustle of old papers in the breeze—all things they might not have paid any attention to under ordinary circumstances but which now added to their uneasiness. The rain soon came, a long, heavy downpour, and they could hear the dripping of water somewhere from the roof. Fortunately their own section of the room remained quite dry, saving them an added inconvenience. But the storm passed at last, their own overstimulated senses no longer responded to the distractions about them, and they finally fell asleep.

In the morning, as the sun broke through the very dirty windows, they arose, but could hardly say they felt rested. They were stiff from sleeping on the hard floor, and the thought of no breakfast and an extremely long hike did nothing to improve their spirits.

They left the house, and looked around outside once more. Further examination of the crawl space convinced them that no one could have been hiding under there while the call was made. They also looked around for footprints, but rain had settled the dust, and nothing had disturbed the ground since. If there had been anyone else there, he must have left before the rain. They checked for wires, too, but Ted's supposition was correct. There wasn't a sign of a telephone pole anywhere in sight. The telephone call in this empty house was as mysterious as the call in the other one.

As they approached the end of the drive, Nelson remarked, "Let's see if we can't figure out what happened to my car. We didn't hear the motor, so that makes me think he must have coasted it out of here. It's downhill from the drive, and there's a long hill on the road below."

"Mm." Ted's sharp eyes were glancing rapidly about. "Hey, what's that across the road?"

"Where?" Nelson's eyes followed Ted's pointing finger. "Say, that's my car, almost hidden in the bushes. Well, what do you know?" He sounded excited, but not especially pleased, and now his tone became almost mournful. "I was hoping the insurance company would get me a better one."

"I wonder if it could have rolled there by itself?" Ted speculated.

"Listen here, my brakes are *good*. They're so tight that even if the *rest* of the car had rolled down the hill, the *brakes* would have stayed right where they were."

Ted smiled, but he was obliged to admit that Nelson was probably right. Not only were the brakes good, but the man who made the call must have deliberately hidden the car to make sure they would be present at the empty house to receive his call later.

"Anyway, we know he wasn't after my dinky little car," said Nelson, disgruntled. "Whatever he's after, it's something bigger than that. Say, Ted, you don't think this man you talked to was Mr. Gray, do you?"

"The man without a dog? I couldn't say, but whatever made you think of him?"

"Oh, I don't know. I was just thinking about all that trouble he took to meet you that one time. How do we know he's through with you yet?"

Ted shook his head. "We can't know for sure, but my feeling is he got everything out of me that he wanted. Regardless of what he's up to, I think I've seen the last of him, as far as what he's doing affecting me."

"Mr. Denning and Mr. Gray couldn't be the same person, could they?"

"No, no, nothing like that. I imagine Mr. Gray was just considering making an investment, and was hoping to get some inside information. That's all legitimate enough, as long as he isn't breaking any laws."

"And I suppose there isn't any law against looking for your dog at night, even if you don't have a dog."

Although Nelson's pride had been injured a little by the failure of the thief to keep his car, they were still glad they were saved from a long hike, and rode happily back to Forestdale, making excellent time.

"But we still don't know for sure whether that house is haunted," Nelson pointed out.

"It will be—by the time *you* tell about it," Ted assured him.

At home once more, Ted washed up and changed his clothes. Then over a rather hurried breakfast he gave his mother some of the details of the night's adventures. After hearing the story she suggested that perhaps he ought to notify the police.

"No, I don't think so," Ted decided thoughtfully, gulping down the last of his breakfast. "I don't think I need police protection, and outside of that I don't think I can do much for the police, or they for me. Sergeant Jeffers already knows about that other telephone call, and if he can't figure that one out, he won't be able to figure this one out, either. I'm a little late. Good-by, Mom."

So much had been happening that Ted had nearly forgotten about Carl's story he had had to kill, but he was reminded of it as Carl came storming into the newspaper office.

"Will you please explain to me what's going on here?" Carl demanded. "I've never run into anything like this in my entire life. Imagine, a whole column of tripe like this, right on the front page. If people want to advertise in our paper, why don't you make them pay for it?"

"Mr. Dobson sometimes uses it," Ted pointed out, "but maybe not a whole column of it, and not on the front page."

Carl's eyes narrowed into slits. "All well and good, Ted. We can't expect to maintain the same efficiency we had while we had a full staff. All I want to know is this: *what happened to my story?*"

"I didn't think we ought to print it."

"Not print it?" Carl's face looked menacing. "Why not?"

Ted's heart was beating more rapidly, not because he was afraid of Carl's threats, but because he wondered what effect his next words would have.

"I didn't think it was right to print the obituary of a man who isn't even dead yet!"

"What!" Carl almost screamed. Then suddenly his legs seemed to collapse under him, and he sank weakly into a chair. "If this is your idea of a joke, Wilford—"

"No, it's no joke. You said Mr. Philip Johnson had died. You're right, Mr. Philip Johnson did die. The only trouble is that it isn't the famous industrial designer named Johnson you wrote your story about."

"Good heavens! Are you sure about that, Ted?"

"Yes, I'm sure. I checked."

"But the names are the same, and the same road—it's out in the country where there aren't any house numbers. Sometimes fathers and sons will have the same names, but I checked that out. I knew Mr. Johnson's father wasn't living, and that he didn't have a son. I didn't feel like checking at the house just then. How'd you catch it, Ted?"

"Well, I knew I'd met Mr. Johnson, and I tried to think back when it was. I remembered it was about three months ago, when he spoke at school. I noticed you said Mr. Johnson had been ill about a year, but that didn't seem right, for he appeared to be in good health when I saw him. So I checked it."

Carl was shaking his head rapidly. "Same name, same road, and some of the other details were the same, too. Who would have thought something like that could happen? And to think it almost got by."

"It could have happened to anybody," said Ted mildly.

"Remember the time we printed a weather report that said the sun was going to come out around 11 P.M.? That was only a typographical error, but this! Why, I'd have been laughed right out of town!"

Carl wasn't angry, or trying to bluster his way out of it. Instead, he had come right out and admitted he'd made a bad mistake, and was grateful to Ted for catching it. Ted felt his respect for Carl rising, and wondered if they couldn't get along together better in the future. Perhaps the same thought was in Carl's mind as he said:

"I know we haven't hit it off so well in the past, Ted. Partly it's been my fault, but partly I think it's because you don't understand the kind of guy I am. A newspaper is run on a rigid time schedule, we have deadlines that have to be met. When I have an appointment I have to be on time, for I can't afford to keep important people waiting. I even have to get home on time, because I live at a rooming house, and if I'm late there's no supper. You think I'm pretty rigid and exacting. Maybe that's the way I naturally am, but maybe it's my work that's helped make me this way."

"That's all well and good," Ted returned, feeling that this might be a good time to try to clear the air, "but sometimes it seems to me you ought to be willing to give a little more of yourself—like last Saturday afternoon, when you knew the paper was in trouble, and you telephoned Miss Monroe you weren't coming in."

"Do you know where I was when I called, Ted? I was down at the capital, cooling my heels for an appointment that didn't come off. I didn't get back to Forestdale till dark."

Like many misunderstandings, this one cleared up when it could be discussed reasonably and calmly. While he and Carl would probably never be big pals, Ted felt they would be more friendly in the future than they had been in the past.

"You've done me a big favor, Ted, and I appreciate it. Maybe I can do something for you. You pulled a booboo when you returned those highway plans to the thief, but I don't see any reason why we should ever print that in the paper."

"But I *want* you to print it," Ted assured him. "If it's news, it belongs in there. I don't want you to cover up just for me."

"Well," said Carl dubiously, "we can't do anything about it right now. My promise to Mr. Montague keeps the lid on that for a while, and maybe by the time the story breaks it won't be up to me to decide any longer."

The morning moved along much as usual. Ted used only part of his lunch hour to eat, and then, returning to the office, checked into the newspaper files for the old story about Everett House. He found the affair was not quite so mysterious as later rumors had made it seem. Mr. Everett had been found afterward, living quietly in the city. He explained that his wife had been incurably ill, and learning it, they had moved out into the country where they could spend their last few months together. When she died, he had returned to the city, moving without notifying his neighbors, whom he described as busybodies. Furthermore, he had the necessary medical certificates to back up his story. As in so many cases, the truth had long ago been forgotten, while the legend remained.

13.

The Sleepy Passenger

THERE WAS good news from Miss Monroe. Her operation had been successful, and she hoped to return to the office in about a week. That was a little soon, perhaps, but Ted knew that her doctor would have a battle on his hands if he tried to keep her away from the office any longer than was absolutely necessary.

Although he was doing his best, Ted had no illusions that he was running the paper as well as Mr. Dobson and Miss Monroe did. Many things that could have gone into the paper were left out because he didn't know how to handle them, or because he didn't have the time or prestige or personal contacts to pursue the stories. Other things involved matters of editorial judgment, to which he did not feel he had the authority to commit the paper. And of course he couldn't even begin to conduct the type of "crusade" for which Mr. Dobson was famous. The *Town Crier* was still readable and conveyed a general feeling of competence, but it lacked the fire and zest its readers had come to expect of it. But now that he knew Miss Monroe would be coming back before long, Ted's spirits rose, and he determined to do his best for the remainder of his term of service.

As he usually did, Nelson dropped in near the close of the day.

"We ought to think about putting you on our pay roll," said Ted jokingly, "if we had a pay roll."

Nelson was chafing over their experience in the haunted house, Ted learned, his chief grievance being that his promises to Ted prevented him from telling anybody about it.

"Don't let that bother you," Ted soothed him. "The longer you have to think about it, the better story you'll be able to make out of it."

"It's good enough the way it is," Nelson grumbled. "The trouble is that you won't let me off the hook until everything's explained, and if there's anything that kills a good ghost story, it's being able to explain it."

There were no new developments on the affair of the empty houses, Ted told him. Nelson, who liked action, wondered if there wasn't anything more they might do to help bring matters to a head.

"I've got an idea that maybe we ought to look up the woman who found the package on the train," Ted suggested.

"What good would that do?"

"I don't know, but the last time I talked with her I didn't realize there was anything wrong about that package. Since then the whole picture's changed. Maybe she caught a glimpse of the man whose package she picked up, or maybe she knows where he got on the train. Possibly she can give us an idea how the packages came to be mixed up. What do you say we drive out to see Mrs. Conway in Brightsville?"

"Right now—before supper?"

"Sure, we can put on the feed bag along the way."

"Oh, you mean list it on the swindle sheet?"

"I suppose it would be all right. We're on newspaper business."

"Then see if you can't get me a set of new tires." Nelson laughed.

They each had telephone calls to make so they would not

be expected home, and then set out. In spite of Ted's "swindle sheet," they stopped at a hamburger stand for supper, which was their favorite manner of eating out. Ted picked up the check but did not add it to his expense account, feeling that he would have to eat no matter where he was, and Nelson refused to accept anything toward his car expenses.

"I'm just in this thing for fun," he stated.

At first Mrs. Conway did not remember them, and it took them a minute or two to explain their errand. Then she invited them in. Her face looked lined, as though she had had many worries on her mind in the last few weeks.

"I hope there wasn't anything wrong about the parcel," she began, as they seated themselves.

"No," Ted assured her, "or at least nothing as far as you're concerned, but there's some doubt that the person who ran the advertisement was the real owner. We thought we'd like to ask you just how the parcels came to be exchanged. Perhaps that might help us settle the matter."

"Were the parcels really exchanged?" Nelson inquired. "Did you lose something, too?"

"Oh, no, I didn't lose anything. If I said I picked up the wrong parcel, that was just my way of expressing it. I was so very much upset the day I found it, and the day after when I returned it, that I didn't make my meaning clear. The truth is that I was very much worried over the illness of my mother. I'm happy to say that she's improving at last, but I'm still staying here with her, as you see.

"It was late Sunday night when I got a telephone call about her illness. My husband agreed that I ought to stay with her for a while, but there was no transportation available until morning. Nevertheless, I didn't get much sleep that night. I kept half-expecting there would be another telephone call about my mother.

"I'm afraid I was very tired the next morning, which was part of the reason for my confusion. The earliest train left about the middle of the morning. Before that I visited several stores which had opened early, and made quite a few purchases—groceries and other things I thought I might need in the next week or two. I put them all in a shopping bag, and it was pretty full.

"On the train it was rather crowded, so I put the shopping bag on the rack overhead. Then, I suppose, being so tired and worried and upset, I must have dozed off. I woke with rather a start, not knowing how long I had slept, and afraid that I had missed my stop. There was a lot of confusion on the train. I didn't understand what it was all about, but I learned later that there was some sort of civic celebration in Forestdale.

"The train was just pulling in, but I didn't know it was Forestdale. My shopping bag had fallen over on the shelf, and some of the parcels had rolled out, but I hurriedly shoved them back into the bag, and started toward the door. Of course I inquired of someone what stop this was, and when I learned it was Forestdale, I went back to my seat. And that's really all I know about it. I found this extra parcel when I arrived at my mother's, and didn't know what to do with it. My mother's condition being what it was, I couldn't do anything about it that day. The next morning I saw the advertisement in the *Town Crier*, and so I came to return it."

"Did you notice anyone on the train," asked Ted, "a man, perhaps, who might have put this parcel up on the rack?"

"No, I don't think I really noticed anyone. There was a man sitting next to me for a while, but I don't believe he was there long. My impression is that he went forward to the smoking car, but I really can't be sure. He wasn't there when I awoke at Forestdale, nor did I see him later."

"Do you think you could describe him?"

"Not very well. I really didn't pay that much attention."

"And you're not sure whether he put a parcel up on the rack?"

"No, I'm afraid I couldn't say. I must have dozed off by that time."

This was about all Mrs. Conway had to tell them, so they thanked her and left after assuring her several times that she hadn't done anything wrong and no trouble was likely to come to her.

"That's one thing that's bothered me," Ted remarked to Nelson as they drove back toward Forestdale. "How did the parcel get into Mrs. Conway's hands? She seems so honest and upset that I don't believe she picked it up intentionally. But if it was such a valuable parcel, wouldn't you think that the owner—or the man who had stolen it—would have been more careful with it? I shouldn't think he would have let it out of his sight."

"With all that confusion on the train," Nelson observed, "he might have been just as upset as Mrs. Conway, knowing he had stolen a valuable set of plans. Maybe he saw her pick up the wrong parcel, but for one reason or another felt he couldn't voice his objections just then. I know *I* wouldn't claim a stolen parcel, if I thought a cop was looking."

Ted shook his head, still dubious. Yet the fact remained that Mr. Denning *had* let the plans get out of his possession, and that he was very anxious to get them back, for he had telephoned the advertisement in to the *Town Crier* not very long after the train had arrived.

"Tell you something," Nelson offered. "It seems to me that this whole case somehow centers around the interchange planned at Milford. You know my aunt lives over in Milford. Why don't we drop out to see her one of these days? She might be able to brief us on what's going on around there."

"It's an idea," Ted agreed.

"When do you want to go? Tomorrow afternoon?"

"I guess that would be as good a time as any for me. Not till about two or three o'clock, though. That Saturday-noon closing time is just a laugh as far as I'm concerned. I'm about two days behind on the mail already."

"Let it go long enough and you can simply drop it in the wastebasket and no one will know the difference. Of course you have to look through it first for checks or orders."

"Oh, I took care of that, first thing."

"Friday night," Nelson observed. "This is our anniversary."

"Anniversary of what?"

"Maybe I ought to call it week-versary. Just a week ago tonight we were graduated."

"Is that all?" said Ted in surprise. "It seems like a million years."

This was the first night since he had started working that Ted had failed to bring home any work from the office. He regretted it now, for it was still fairly early when he arrived home. He was glad, however, to find a letter from Ronald waiting for him, and he read it eagerly.

Ronald, of course, had heard nothing so far about the missing plans. Ted thought this might be a good time to acquaint him with the facts of the case, and he got out his portable and ran a sheet of paper into it. He outlined the whole story, beginning with that first telephone call of Mr. Denning's, about placing an ad in the lost-and-found. When he had finished with the visit they had just paid to Mrs. Conway, Ted felt he had covered the case pretty well, though sketchily. Writing Ronald like this helped to bring the facts into some logical order in his own mind.

Ted could not escape the feeling that he was the center of a vast spiderweb of intrigue, far more complicated and entangled than he could understand. What was it all about? Was there any hope of finding the guilty party and recovering the plans? The facts were all in front of him, but they didn't mean very much unless you could draw some conclusions from them, even tentative conclusions. Maybe that was because there were so many details it was hard to fit them all into a logical pattern. But even if he couldn't hope to solve the whole mystery all at once, weren't there at least a few pieces he could solve? Those telephone calls, for instance . . .

Suddenly Ted had an inspiration, and almost ran to the telephone. He asked the long-distance operator for Mr. Montague's home number.

After a short delay, Mr. Montague came to the phone.

"Mr. Montague, this is Ted Wilford."

"Who?" asked the state auditor, as though he had never heard the name before.

"Ted Wilford of the Forestdale *Town Crier*."

"Oh." Mr. Montague sounded as though he wasn't sure he had ever heard of the *Town Crier* either, or if so that he never wanted to hear of it again.

"Mr. Montague, I'd like to ask you a question."

"Well, go ahead," he answered impatiently. "I hope you have some information that will help recover the plans."

"No, nothing like that. Mr. Montague, when you left on your vacation, did you order your telephone disconnected?"

"Yes, I did. I live in an apartment, and I didn't want people calling repeatedly without getting an answer, and the bell perhaps disturbing other residents. Is that all you wanted?"

"Yes, that's all."

"Well, I hope the information is of some use to you," said Mr. Montague sarcastically. "Hereafter please use my home number only for important calls. You can reach me at the office for trivialities like this."

But Ted, as he hung up, was too jubilant to take much notice of Mr. Montague's criticism. He felt he had uncovered an important clue. A telephone man had probably been present in Mr. Montague's apartment at about the very time the plans were stolen.

14.

The Milford Speculator

NELSON APPEARED at the office at two-thirty, and Ted, giving up hope of ever getting finished, decided not to try. Instead, he packed a folder full of work to take home, hoping he might find some time for it over the weekend.

"Just one week more till Miss Monroe comes back," he pointed out.

"And then you'll have the rest of the summer to try to regain your sanity," Nelson added.

As they headed north out of Forestdale, Ted said, "We pass through North Ridge, don't we?"

"We can if you want to."

"Well, then, let's stop off at Ken Kutler's. I haven't seen his new home, and he's asked me to stop in sometime. You haven't met his wife yet, have you?"

"No. Is she nice?"

"Oh, yes. The quiet type. But I think she knows just how to keep Ken in line without his even realizing she's doing it."

"Think we'll find Ken home? And if so, then what? You acting on a hunch?"

"Call it that, if you want to. It's about those mysterious telephone calls. I still can't explain them, but I have the feeling it would have to be someone very familiar with telephone work—say an employee of the telephone company—to arrange the setup."

"Maybe, though I don't see how even a telephone employee can work a telephone without wires," Nelson maintained. "But you might be right. He'd have a better chance to do it than anyone else would. Still, suppose you did have a long list of employees. How would you know which is the right one? You couldn't check on all of them."

"I know. That's why I thought maybe Ken would have some ideas."

"This looks like it could turn into a pretty big story, Ted. Are you sure you ought to work along with Ken this way? After all, you're working for different papers, and Ron and Ken used to battle each other every inch of the way, even though they were friends."

"I suppose ideally I oughtn't to, but what else can I do? Carl would never follow up on an idea like this, and I'm tied down to the office. Besides, I don't think the telephone company would let me check on their employees—they'd think I was just being nosy. But they'd trust Ken, for he's been around for a long time. So as long as it's something I can't use myself, why not give Ken a crack at it? After all, I was the one who gave the plans away, so I've got a strong interest in getting them back, if I possibly can."

Both Ken and his wife were at home, and glad to see them.

"Pretty nice home you have," Ted observed. "Quite a bit larger than your old place."

"We needed a larger one. This may be the last time you'll be visiting just the *two* of us."

"Well, congratulations!" Ted returned. "I didn't mean to pry. I just thought—"

"You weren't prying. I've been bursting with the news, but my wife's been trying to calm me down. She's just as excited as I am, but she doesn't think I have to tell *everybody*. She doesn't think everyone would be interested."

But these visitors were interested. "If it's a boy," Nelson

inquired, "are you going to raise him to be a newspaperman?"

"Not if I can help it! I wouldn't wish that on my worst enemy." Ken grinned. "But the chances are he'll be just as bullheaded as I am, and become a newspaperman anyway."

They all laughed, and Ted said:

"Speaking of newspaper work, I have a little idea I wanted to talk to you about in connection with these highway plans."

Ken held up a restraining hand. "Just a moment, Ted. I want to be perfectly frank with you. I've been following up my own angle on this case. So far it hasn't led me anywhere, but it still might. Is it understood that whatever you've got to tell me comes with no strings attached—that I can use it in any way I think fit?"

"Oh, yes," Ted assured him. "There aren't any strings as far as I'm concerned. I can't get the story myself, so if you're able to dig it out that's all right with me."

Ted, with some prompting from Nelson, quickly covered the details Ken was unfamiliar with. He had to smile when they told about the haunted house, for haunted houses seem very amusing in the daytime.

"And now what's the hunch, Ted?" asked Ken.

"I don't know whether it's much of a hunch," said Ted slowly, "but it occurred to me that maybe Mr. Montague had his telephone disconnected, as long as he was leaving for a month's vacation, and wouldn't return to his city apartment at all until the fall session of the Legislature. So I called him to check, and he admitted it. That means a telephone man was probably there at about the time the plans were stolen."

"Would he have come to the apartment?" asked Nelson. "Couldn't the telephone be disconnected at the central office?"

"I'm not sure," Ken answered. "If it had been a party line, I think a lineman would have to come out. I suppose service could be disconnected either at the pole or inside the apartment building. But I believe the telephone company often make a practice of checking the lines and equipment at such a time to make sure they're in good shape. And of course if they were actually going to remove the instrument, a lineman would have to get into the apartment. I think it's a fair assumption that a telephone man was there."

"Well, it seems to me," Ted went on, "with all these mysterious telephone calls, a telephone man is a logical suspect."

"Wait a minute," Nelson interrupted. "Which telephone company are you talking about? The Forestdale company covers a pretty big area, but it doesn't reach the city, or anywhere near it."

"No," Ted continued. "I thought it might be a Forestdale telephone employee who went to Mr. Montague's apartment pretending to be an employee of their telephone company."

"Well, that's pretty good," Nelson muttered. "A telephone employee disguising himself as a telephone employee. That shouldn't have been very hard."

Ken was considering all this information very carefully. "I admit, Ted, that I was approaching the case from an entirely different angle. But you might have something. I'll start checking into it this afternoon."

"We don't like to break up your Saturday," Ted objected.

"Oh, I don't care. My wife's planned on my cleaning rugs, so she'll be the only one to mind."

They left soon afterward. At about five o'clock they arrived in Milford. Nelson's aunt, Mrs. Evans, was delighted to see him, and welcomed Ted with as much enthusiasm as though he were her own nephew.

She took it for granted they would stay for supper, and they were happy to agree because the smell of fresh bread, a pot of stew steaming on the stove, and home-grown vegetables, homemade butter, and some of her own canned fruits were making their mouths water.

Only as the meal ended did Ted feel like bringing up the

topic which had brought them there. At the first mention of the thruway, he saw their faces cloud, and realized that this was not a particularly pleasant subject for them.

"I don't know why they have to bring the highway through here," Mrs. Evans maintained. "There must be lots of other places they could build it. We've got nothing to gain from it. Our children have grown and married—flown the coop, as we call it—and your uncle and I had figured on settling down to a quiet life. It won't be much of a quiet life, with a busy highway running past our front door."

"Well, they have to build it somewhere," said Nelson mildly.

"But not here," Mr. Evans put in. "It isn't just a question of inconvenience. It would probably mean the end of farming in this whole area. You see, we're on high ground here, and the road would have to cut through the hills. That's going to mean a lowering of the water table and might put an end to farming altogether. At least that's what the farmers think. It's happened in other places, and it could happen here."

"But there must be some people who feel just the opposite about it," Ted suggested.

"Not farmers," said Mr. Evans firmly. "Outsiders, who think they can buy up our land cheap and turn it to commercial purposes—for service stations, motels, and restaurants—are the ones in favor of it. There's been someone around here already, buying up options as he calls it."

"What do you intend to do if the highway comes through here?" Nelson questioned.

"Why, I suppose we'd have to get out," his aunt returned. "If we couldn't farm we couldn't stay. Anyway, I'm not sure we'd want to even if we could. It wouldn't be the kind of retirement we'd dreamed about. We're thinking of moving to Forestdale if we can find a house to rent, but they seem to be very scarce."

Ted's thoughts had jumped rapidly to another tangent. "You say there has been a man around here already, buying up options? What did he say? Did he tell you the highway was certain to go through here?"

He was looking at Mr. Evans, but the farmer shook his head. "It was my wife who talked with him. She'll tell you."

"No, he didn't exactly say the highway was going through here. He said he thought it *might*, and was willing to take a chance."

"Then you didn't give him an option?"

"Certainly not. We're not going to believe the highway's coming through here just on his say-so. The last we'd heard, the governor hadn't made up his mind yet."

"But I must say his proposition sounds very generous and straightforward," Mr. Evans added. "The figure he offered was more than the present value of the farm, and probably more than we'd get from the government if we went through condemnation proceedings. He said we'd have to make up our minds soon, though. If he couldn't get this farm, he was going to buy other properties nearby. At least, as I told Polly, it wouldn't do any harm just to talk to the man again."

Ted's excitement was mounting. "Do you know this man's name, Mrs. Evans?"

"Why, yes. Mr. Caldwell, I think it was. I have his card somewhere around."

"And would you be willing to talk to this man again, Mrs. Evans—tonight? Nelson could station himself outside and get the license number, and I think I could hide in the bedroom and hear everything that was said. It might help give me the information I'm after."

"I guess we could do that, Ted, if it would help you," she agreed, "and probably we ought to talk to him again anyway, just for our own benefit. But we aren't going to sign anything tonight—I'm going to make that clear to him."

"We'll never touch pen to paper without consulting a lawyer first," her husband vowed.

Mrs. Evans phoned Mr. Caldwell, saying that her husband would be at home that evening, and asking if he'd care to stop by to explain his proposition further. He agreed to be there within an hour.

As the time approached, they took up their stations. Nelson had previously moved his own car out of sight, behind the barn. Ted, from the bedroom, could not risk a view of the visitor as he arrived, but thought that he might be able to get a glimpse of him as he left.

Mr. Caldwell arrived on time. "Good evening, Mrs. Evans. How do you do, Mr. Evans," he said in a pleasant voice that sounded strangely familiar to Ted. "Your wife tells me that you're considering my proposition."

"Just mulling it over in my mind," said Mr. Evans cautiously. "We won't decide anything tonight."

"Take your time, Mr. Evans," said Mr. Caldwell, although his voice sounded a little disappointed. "I don't want to rush you, although you realize that I have other possibilities developing, too."

"Please sit down, Mr. Caldwell, and tell my husband all about it," Mrs. Evans invited.

He sat down and began to talk, and as he outlined his plan Ted had to admit it sounded both fair and honest.

"But what if the highway doesn't come through here?" asked Mr. Evans. "Then what happens?"

"Then, Mr. Evans, I'll simply drop my option. Your farm would be useless to me in that case. You will keep the option money for your trouble. That's the gamble I'm willing to take."

"Do we just have your word on that?"

"Mr. Evans, you needn't take my word on anything. It's all down in the contract."

"Of course we'd want to consult a lawyer," Mrs. Evans pointed out.

"I strongly urge that you do that, Mrs. Evans. This is a perfectly legal document, and I think it's important that you thoroughly understand it."

"But if your price is really a fair one," Mr. Evans came in, "how do you expect to make a profit?"

"The price I am offering, Mr. Evans, is a fair one *now*. After the land is commercially developed, it will be worth more. That's where I expect to make my profit."

"Well, I don't see how we can lose on a proposition like yours," Mr. Evans mused. "If the highway comes through, we'd want to sell anyway, and we might as well sell to you at your generous price—I doubt if we'll get any better offer. And if the highway doesn't come through, we stay, and we're ahead the option money."

"Believe me, you can't lose," said Mr. Caldwell earnestly. "I'm the only one who can lose. I represent a group of investors who can afford to risk their money, taking chances that a small individual doesn't dare to take."

"Well, we'll think it over and let you know next week," Mr. Evans promised.

"Do that," said Mr. Caldwell, rising to his feet.

His voice remained vaguely familiar, but Ted was still unable to place it. He thought he'd better risk that glimpse, and managed it just as Mr. Caldwell was about to open the front door. He was completely surprised.

Nelson came in after the visitor had left. He and Ted expressed their thanks to the elderly couple, and also left.

On the road at last, Nelson exclaimed, "I got the license number. Now we'll be able to find out who it is."

"Never mind that. It isn't important now."

"You mean you already know who it is?" Nelson demanded. "Well, come on, tell me."

"His name's Mr. Lamont, and he's an employee of the Highway Department. I've met him at the office. He came to ask about the missing plans."

"You mean an employee of the Highway Department has been speculating in land along the right of way? Wow! What do you intend doing about it?"

"I don't know just yet," said Ted tiredly. "First I want to give this a long, long think."

15.

A Question of Ethics

MONDAY MORNING was the usual rat race, with the customary rush to beat the noon deadline. By now Ted was becoming used to it, and learned that if he just didn't let himself get flustered by the continual flood of details and interruptions, everything would probably turn out all right.

The matter of the Milford options had been on his mind all day Sunday, and by now he had reached a tentative decision on what he was going to do, although he still didn't know just when or how he was going to accomplish it. Like Ted, it was something direct and candid; he hated beating about the bush, engaging in subterfuges, pretending the situation was different from what he knew it to be.

The opportunity presented itself unexpectedly when Mr. Lamont walked into the office. Having reached his decision, Ted was glad to see him, although he kept one eye on the clock with his deadline approaching.

"How are you, Ted?" said Mr. Lamont cordially. "Just thought I'd drop in for a minute to see if there are any new developments about the missing plans."

"Well, yes, there is one new development," said Ted, swinging around.

"Indeed?" Mr. Lamont's eyes grew cold. "May I ask what it is?"

"Yes. I've learned that you've been speculating on options in Milford, using the name Mr. Caldwell."

"Ted, I—" He started to bluster, but saw at once there was no use denying it, so instead he asked carefully, "What makes you think so?"

"Mr. and Mrs. Evans are relatives of a friend of mine."

Mr. Lamont sank into a chair. "Ted, I want you to know just what the situation is. First of all, I wasn't trying to cheat Mr. and Mrs. Evans, or anyone else. I was offering them a legitimate business proposition. They wouldn't have lost anything, and they might have had considerable to gain."

"That may be true with respect to Mr. and Mrs. Evans and the other farmers," Ted agreed. "But I'm not sure it's an ethical thing for a public official to engage in speculations the way you're doing."

All Mr. Lamont's open friendliness had disappeared, and Ted saw him now as a bitter, beaten-down man.

"I want to explain the whole thing to you, Ted, so you'll understand my point of view. I wonder if you know what it's like to hold a political job like mine. I haven't had a raise in three years, or a promotion in five, although I believe I am legitimately entitled to them. Do you know what my crime is? I vote the wrong way. So far I've managed to hang on, but I have a feeling that after the next election I'll be let out, and replaced by someone else who votes the way he's told. Oh, I know technically I'm under civil service, which is why I've hung on this long, but when the big bosses decide they want to get rid of you, they can always find some excuse.

"Now about the Milford situation. Maybe you've got the wrong idea about what sort of official I am. I'm not high up in the department. I'm just a glorified office clerk. Of course I knew about the plans being drawn up, and there was the usual office scuttlebutt about whether the Milford interchange was going to be built, or whether the thruway would avoid Milford altogether. But as I said, I'm only a clerk, and I haven't the faintest idea what the governor is finally going to decide to do about it.

"But just on my own hunch—on my own judgment of whether or not the Milford interchange would be a good thing—I determined to take a plunge. It seemed to me that the most logical thing would be to go ahead and build the interchange, and so I decided to play it that way. I've invested almost everything I can raise on options, backing up my hunch. Of course it's a gamble, and I could be wrong— I know that. But looking at it the other way, what does the future hold for me if I stay on in the Highway Department? From my point of view it looks pretty bleak, in spite of the fact that I've been there nearly fifteen years. If I could just make a private killing, I could resign from the department before I'm fired, and wash my hands of the whole mess.

"You're still very young, and maybe this doesn't sound right to you. But let me tell you that what I'm doing is no different from the things everybody else does, or would do if they had the chance."

He waited a moment, but Ted said nothing.

"May I ask you what you intend to do about it?"

"I don't know yet," said Ted briefly.

"Print it in the paper?"

"I can't tell yet. I'm going to get some advice from a person I trust."

"Well, Ted, I'm not going to plead with you. But I will point out that you have it in your power to ruin my career— or what's left of it. I think you ought to consider long and carefully before you decide to do that."

He left, and Ted tried to return his attention to the pressing business at hand. His story on Mr. Lamont had already been written—he had carefully avoided all reference to the missing plans in order to keep his promise to Mr. Montague

—but he hadn't yet turned it in to the printer. He felt badly in need of advice before making a final decision. There was no use asking Carl; he would say, "If it's true, print it," and that would have been the end of it.

But Ted didn't feel he could handle such a serious story so casually. He knew, as Mr. Lamont had pointed out, that this would probably ruin his career. And he wasn't at all sure that Mr. Lamont had broken any law. The corrupt practices act forbids a state official to use his public knowledge for private gain. But if Mr. Lamont did not have, as he claimed, any inside knowledge of the route the highway would follow, but was merely engaged in personal speculation, he might be operating within the letter of the law.

However, even though it might not be illegal, what Mr. Lamont had done was certainly unethical—or at least a great many people would think so. Is the cry, "Everybody else does it," a legitimate excuse? Ted often wished there was a hard-and-fast line between right and wrong that everyone could observe, but he was learning to accept the fact that this often isn't so.

Earlier that morning Ted had put through a call to Ken. Since Ken was not at his office, Ted had left a message to have him call back. The call came through at about eleven o'clock.

"Hi, Ted, how's everything going?"

"All right, I guess."

"Those deadlines sure creep up on you, don't they?" Ken laughed, then waited to hear what Ted had wanted to tell him.

"I had something I wanted to ask you, Ken. Suppose you knew that a state official had done something which might not be illegal, but was unethical, would you use the story?"

"It's something related to his public life, not his private life?"

"Yes."

"And you're sure of your facts?"

"Yes. I've got witnesses to some of the things he did, and he admitted it to me afterward privately."

"Just a minute, Ted. The fact you've got witnesses is all right, but don't use anything about what he admitted to you privately. He could deny it afterward and you'd find yourself really in the soup."

"Then you think it's all right to use the story?"

"Certainly use it," said Ken bluntly.

"It might hurt his career—"

"He knew what he was doing and took his chances. If public opinion condemns him, it's because the public feels he hasn't conducted himself the way a public official ought to."

"He says everybody else does it."

"If people criticize him, it's because everybody else *doesn't* do it, and they feel a person in his position shouldn't either. That's the kind of alibi people drag up to excuse themselves for almost anything they want to do."

"Well, all right," Ted agreed reluctantly. "I guess I'll use it, then, but it isn't exactly the kind of story I like."

"I know, Ted, it's a dirty story, but you'll get your share of those in the newspaper business. So you found out that someone in the Highway Department has been speculating in land at Milford—"

"Now how did you know that?" Ted demanded, somewhat annoyed.

Ken laughed. "Oh, it wasn't very hard to figure out. It was an obvious point of attack to check on land speculations at Milford, to see if the thief had been trying to cash in on his knowledge. That's the angle I've been following, but it hasn't gotten me anywhere. So far as I was able to learn, the companies speculating there were legitimate concerns, and I wasn't able to learn the name of anyone behind the scenes. I knew you were following up the highway story, and you told me Saturday you were going to Milford. From the questions you just asked me it became clear that you had been able to come up with the name of the man, though I hadn't been able to get it."

"You're not suggesting that this man may have stolen the plans?"

"No, Ted, and from what you've told me I don't think it very likely. Apparently the thief was too clever to speculate at Milford. He could have speculated anywhere along the whole course of the highway, and of course that would be too difficult to check out."

"Are you going to use the story?" asked Ted.

"No, Ted, I'm not. For one thing I've got less than an hour till my deadline, and I don't think I could find out the man's name in that time. For another thing, I wouldn't have known it was some official in the Highway Department if you hadn't practically told me. No, it's your story, Ted, and it ought to be a good one. I'll have to congratulate you on it."

"Are you getting anywhere on that telephone-employee angle, Ken?"

"Still checking, Ted. I'd rather not say anything more about that just now."

"And you still don't know how those telephone calls were made without wires?"

"Forget it, Ted. There had to be wires," and Ken hung up.

In the light of what Ken had advised him, Ted looked his story over once more and made a few changes. Then he took it in to the printer. He still didn't feel quite right about it. However, it was a story, and a good one, and it gave Ted a certain feeling of pride to be one jump ahead of Ken Kutler. It was certainly decent of Ken not to try to use the story himself. But there was still that telephone-employee business. Ken sounded as if he might be on to something there, and

Ted wondered what it was. Even though the tip had come from Ted, that would be Ken's story when he got it.

Once again Nelson came in before closing time. He was beginning to get bored with himself, and was looking around for something to do.

"This town's as dead as a dodo. There's nothing stirring anywhere, not even a good, strong breeze. It's only when I come down to the newspaper here that I get any excitement at all because you usually manage to get me stirred up. If it wasn't for the senior picnic coming up I'd do something drastic—like going to work."

"Get your story ready," Ted advised him. "Maybe you'll be able to tell them about your night in a haunted house."

"No fooling, Ted? You mean something's due to pop off?"

"I wouldn't know, but Ken's sure beginning to sound like it," and he explained about Ken's call.

"Say, Ted," said Nelson, recollecting, "I knew I had something to tell you. I had a call from Aunt Polly today. They gave Mr. Caldwell an option on their farm!"

"They what?" Ted demanded, frozen. He seriously questioned whether a contract signed with a fictitious name would be legally binding.

"Yes. They talked to their lawyer, and he said it was all right, and the price was probably better than they could get anywhere else. So they jumped right in. Other farmers around there have signed up, too, and they were afraid of getting left out in the cold."

"Let me get this straight. Your aunt and uncle gave *Mr. Caldwell* an option on their farm?"

"Well, no, not if you're going to be technical. They signed the contract with a real-estate firm. Mr. Caldwell was only acting as an agent. I know you said his real name is Mr. Lamont, but maybe Caldwell is the real name and Lamont the phony. Anyway, as long as he didn't sign the contract himself, it must be all right."

Yes, it was probably legal enough, Ted thought. Anyway, the lawyer ought to know. Nevertheless, his face showed something of his dismay.

"What's the matter, Ted? You look like the bottom just dropped out of the world. Even if Mr. Lamont has been speculating in land when he shouldn't, it doesn't have anything to do with my aunt, does it?"

"No, I suppose not," Ted agreed reluctantly. "I guess it's mostly a matter of how you look at things. I just don't feel that you ought to deal with a man like Mr. Lamont if you can help it."

"They didn't really know what kind of man he was, and as long as the lawyer said it was O.K.—"

No, they hadn't known, Ted thought, but by tomorrow everyone was going to know, when they'd read his story. He was still glad to have an exclusive story, but wished it could have been about something else.

The telephone rang. Ted was busy at the adding machine totaling up the day's receipts from subscriptions and advertising, pretending that he knew more about double-entry bookkeeping than he did.

"Want to take that, Nel? Make like an editor."

With a good deal of pride, Nelson took the receiver from the cradle, convinced that everything that went on in a newspaper office was momentous, and some of the importance was rubbing off on him. Ted heard his end of the conversation:

"*Town Crier* office. . . . You what? . . . Yes, ma'am, I'd be very happy to. It's exactly eight minutes to five. . . . That's right. Thank you for calling." He hung up the receiver and almost exploded. "Great guns! She wanted to know what time it was! Do people call up their newspaper for tripe like that?"

"You don't know the half of it." Ted grinned. "You ought to be around here for a whole day sometime. I sometimes wonder how Miss Monroe ever manages to get things done. The other day a woman called to tell me she thought she smelled smoke, and wondered if I knew where it was coming from. And they're always calling about the last-minute national news, even though we don't have a wire service. In a way I like it, though. It shows that people really think of the newspaper as the center of things in the community."

With the day's work done, Nelson expected they would leave. Instead, Ted sat down again, looking thoughtful. When Nelson inquired the reason, Ted explained:

"I'm still thinking about that empty house. What was it used for, what was the purpose of all that?"

"Mr. Denning just used it as a place where he could get the plans back from you, didn't he?"

"That's what I thought at first, but now I don't think so any more. He wouldn't have had very much time to arrange it. He lost the plans when the train pulled into Forestdale last Monday morning, and not very long after that he phoned in his ad. How could he have arranged for the empty house and the telephone in such a short time?"

"He didn't have to arrange everything just then, did he? You didn't actually call him back until late in the afternoon."

"No, but he couldn't know that. A newspaper often will call back immediately to verify an ad. He had to have everything ready in case I did that. What I think is that he already had the empty house all set up for some other purpose. Then when he lost the plans he had to use it to get the plans back."

"What do you think he was using the empty house for?"

"I haven't any idea. But my point is that if he needed an

empty house before that, maybe he still needed it afterward. Of course he didn't dare use that house any longer, once we were on to him. So how do we know he didn't look around for another empty house?"

"Where's he going to find one?" Nelson countered. "He was just lucky. He found a house that had been sold, but one the new owner wouldn't be able to move into for a month. That wasn't likely to happen again. And I don't think he could find a house to rent. You know how bad the housing shortage is. When a family moves out, sometimes the next family will move in the very same day, or the following day at the latest."

"How about buying a new house?"

"He wouldn't buy a new house just to carry on his swindle, would he? Anyway, how could he? Buying a house would mean lawyers and banks and maybe going through the courts. If he was trying to keep his name out of it, he'd never be able to get away with that. Anyway, what makes you think he's still operating in the Forestdale area? He could be anywhere in the state by now."

"No, I don't think so," said Ted slowly. "Remember he's doing something with those telephone calls. Maybe that means he has to stay in the area served by the Forestdale telephone company. I don't think he could get away with this in the middle of town, so that means an empty house somewhere around the outskirts. Now how would he go about finding an empty house that he needed?"

"Oh, that's easy," Nelson kidded. "He'd look up the advertisements in the *Town Crier*."

Ted looked excited. "Maybe you just meant that to be funny, but you may have hit it just the same. Let's see what our last few issues had to offer."

None of the recent issues advertised any houses for rent. There were, however, a number of houses for sale. Most of these Ted felt were impossible, because they were in the main part of town. But he was particularly attracted toward a new, expensive development out on Liggett Road.

"That could be it!" he exclaimed.

"What are you going to do now?"

"Call the real-estate company and see what they've got to say."

After the call was over, Ted explained to Nelson what he had learned. "They've got a dozen new homes out there, but most of them aren't completed yet. I don't think they would do—the workmen are still out there. A couple of completed ones are being shown to the public, so I don't think they would do, either. How could Mr. Denning use them, when he never knew at what time the real-estate agent might bring out a client? But there's one completed home that isn't being shown because it's under option."

"More options?" asked Nelson.

"Sure, and I'll bet you that's the ticket. Mr. Denning couldn't find a house to rent, and he couldn't buy one. But he could take out an option on one, which means he'd be able to use it for a month. Options are more informal, and don't go through the long legal channels a sale does. He could get away with that, using a false name."

"Well, what are we going to do about it?"

"I'd like to go out there tonight and watch that empty house."

"After dark?"

"Certainly after dark, if we're going to stand any chance of finding out what's going on."

"Sounds like an adventure to me," Nelson agreed.

They left the office in some excitement. Behind them the presses were still thumping, printing the first big story Ted had ever handled by himself.

16.

Footsteps in an Empty House

THE HOUSE on Liggett Road was some distance from the other homes, located around a small bend and sheltered by large oaks which had been left in their old positions. It seemed to Ted that the decision to spare the old trees was responsible for the somewhat peculiar layout of the street and development. Trees like these took many decades to grow, and probably added thousands of dollars to the value of the lots.

Their car was concealed off the main road, and they approached the development on foot. Nearing the house, they left the road, and made their way in the shadow of the heavy shrubbery. Care had been taken in building to preserve as much of the natural beauty as possible.

"Some houses," Nelson murmured. "These are even better than that first empty house."

"Yes, I guess they're out of our class, for a few years at least. It looks like the builder wasn't sparing any expense when he built these. A nice spot for retired millionaires."

They neared the suspicious house from the rear, and approached as close as they could and still remain concealed by the shrubs. It was nearly night now, except for a faint glow in the western sky. The house lay dark, quiet, and deserted some fifty feet in front of them.

"How long are we going to wait?" asked Nelson.

"As long as we can."

"And then if we don't get anything?"

"I don't know. I haven't thought that far ahead yet."

There was certainly no sign of life in the house in front of them. The doors were closed, though the evening was warm, and the windows were unshuttered and unshaded. The panes caught and reflected the glow of the rising moon. Most of the birds had gone to sleep, although a bat or a nighthawk swung low overhead and silently sped away. Except for the hum of summer insects, everything was perfectly still. There was nothing to suggest that this was anything except what it appeared to be: a new, still-unoccupied house.

"Nobody around, either inside or out, I guess," Nelson observed, as their vigil stretched out.

"Nobody on the outside, anyway," Ted agreed.

"If there were anybody in there, what would he be doing, anyway? Watching television in the dark?"

"Some television set. It'd have to be powered on batteries. There aren't any electric wires strung up to the house."

The time dragged on. And then, sometime after ten o'clock, they heard a telephone ring, muffled but still distinct. It was coming from the empty house.

"You going to try to get in and answer it?" asked Nelson.

"Nothing doing. That's where I made my mistake last time. We're just here to watch and see what happens."

"Looks like nobody's going to answer," Nelson added, as the telephone continued to ring.

"Who's there to answer? There's nobody home. Well, what do you make of it? Another telephone, and no wires."

"What's the matter, you old-fashioned or something? You think telephones need wires?"

At last the telephone stopped ringing, as though the person calling had grown tired of waiting. Around them everything was still once more, except for a faint breeze that rustled the leaves.

"I don't see how that telephone call could have come from outside," Nelson pointed out. "There just aren't any wires anywhere. Do you think there's somebody in that house, ringing the bell himself?"

"What would be the purpose?"

"I don't know—maybe to give us a scare."

"I wouldn't think so—why would they want to make us suspicious? Anyway, nobody knows we're here."

They looked around apprehensively, but their place of concealment seemed to be secure.

"Well, what now?" asked Nelson, standing up to stretch a little, for he had been crouched down watching through the leaves.

"I guess we'll have to go home. We can't stay here much longer, and it doesn't look as though anything more is going to happen. But we'll be back—tomorrow night."

"How do you know this house has anything to do with Mr. Denning?"

"The ringing telephone pretty well proves that, doesn't it?"

"Well, O.K., we can keep on watching, but it's going to be a long, cold winter."

Ted's story came out the next morning. He had placed it on the front page, but near the bottom, displacing a less-important story which was moved to a back page. It wasn't a very important story as far as Forestdale was concerned, for Mr. Lamont wasn't a resident there, nor were the local people closely involved with the Milford interchange.

But if it was not a sensation in Forestdale, where the readers hardly realized what an impressive scoop Ted had, the story created a furor elsewhere. The big daily papers are always alert to the possibility that a person in public office has misused his office. And in this case there was something more, an undercurrent that caught even Ted rather off guard. The suggestion was there that possibly a group of favored persons had been given some inside information about the road plans. This could lead to an even bigger story, and the dailies hopped on it.

Ted was busy for an hour that morning answering calls from the big papers. They wanted to check on his facts, and Ted tried to be as helpful as he could, although true to his promise to Mr. Montague he said nothing about the missing plans. One reporter told him that Mr. Montague was being asked for a statement, but declined to say anything until he could consult with the governor.

Among the telephone callers was Ken Kutler.

"You did a fine job, Ted," he congratulated him. "I think you handled it just perfectly."

This praise from a newspaperman meant a great deal to Ted, and more than made up for the indifference of the local townspeople, who still didn't realize what Ted had done. They probably thought he had copied the story from one of the big papers, Ted told himself.

That night Ted and Nelson drove out to the empty house. As before, they parked their car off the main road and approached the house in the same roundabout fashion. The sun was fast sinking below the horizon, and long shadows were beginning to merge into each other, until they formed a solid dark blanket. The boys believed they had reached their place of concealment without being seen.

"Wonder if that telephone will ring again tonight?" Nelson speculated.

"We'll just have to wait and see."

Gradually complete darkness and an all-pervading quiet settled over the isolated development. They wondered if they were faced with another long vigil, with nothing to show for it except a ringing telephone they couldn't explain.

But soon they discovered that this night was going to be different from the preceding one in one respect, at least.

"Listen, what's that?" asked Ted cautiously.

Nelson listened just as carefully. "It's hard to make out, but it sounds to me like footsteps inside the empty house."

"That's the way I made it out, too. At least this time we're sure somebody's inside the house. I wonder if he could have been there yesterday?"

"If he was, he should have answered his telephone."

Suddenly they caught a faint flicker of light upon the windowpane. At first they thought it was the moon, but then the light began to move about.

"He's got a flashlight," Nelson pointed out, "and he's got his hand over the end, so it doesn't show much."

"Now he's going on into another room. It looks like he's searching for something."

The light soon went out, but they could not be sure whether the searcher had switched it off or had merely moved on into another room where they could not see him. At least they caught no further glimpse of the light, nor could they catch any more footsteps, much as they strained their eyes and ears. To all appearances, the empty house was once more quiet and deserted. Yet this time they felt the tension mounting inside them. Both doors were within their range of vision, and they knew no one had left.

Nelson moved uneasily, and kept glancing backward.

"What are you doing?" asked Ted in a very soft whisper, afraid to raise his voice above the barest audible tone.

"Just checking. I keep getting the feeling that someone is creeping up behind us."

However, he discovered nothing, decided it was just nerves, and concentrated his attention on the house. Time passed, but nothing changed, except that the moon was rising higher in the sky.

"Do you think he may have left by a window on the other side of the house?" Nelson whispered.

"Don't count on it. I think he's sitting there in the dark—waiting for something."

If the person inside the house thought there was something worth waiting for, then it was worth their while to wait, too, although the hour was growing late. The air was cool and damp, and they were beginning to grow stiff. Nevertheless, they kept themselves as quiet as possible and did not relax their vigilance, their nerves steeled to meet whatever new development the night might bring them. They knew they were dealing with a criminal—an important criminal—and who could tell what a criminal might do, especially if he thought he was cornered?

The moon continued to rise, casting changing shadows beyond the tall oak trees. It was very still, and nothing further disturbed the quiet of the house.

"Maybe he's waiting for morning," said Nelson, trying to relieve the tension a little. "Maybe he fell asleep."

"I don't think there's any bed in there."

"What's that matter? Tramps will sometimes crawl into an empty house to sleep, just to get under shelter."

"This guy's no tramp. I never heard of a tramp with a telephone."

And then at last their vigil was rewarded as they heard more footsteps—but not from the empty house. They were coming from the other way, along the deserted sidewalk. Someone was approaching. They looked hastily about, but felt that their hiding place was secure. The person approaching probably had no idea they were there, and he wasn't going to stumble into them by accident.

At first they couldn't tell who it was, though they could dimly make out his dark form. He was keeping to the shadows as much as he could. However, there was one bright, moonlit patch, between the shadow of the oaks and the house, that he could not avoid, and he started across it hurriedly.

Ted found his excitement mounting until he felt almost ready to burst. He knew, from Nelson's heavy breathing beside him, that he had also recognized the man. They could not take a chance on speaking until the man had stepped inside the apparently unlocked house.

"Why, that was Mr. Gray!" Nelson exclaimed.

"Yes," Ted confirmed, "the man who pretended he'd lost his dog."

"So he's the one we were after all the time."

"We can't be sure about that yet. Anyway, I'll bet he didn't lose his dog way out here."

There was a moment's delay, and then a light went on in the front room.

"What did he do, light a kerosene lamp?" asked Nelson.

"Kerosene lamp, your grandmother! That's an electric light!"

"An electric light without wires," Nelson moaned. "Before I just thought I was crazy, but now I'm sure of it."

They could not see what was going on inside the room. They supposed the two persons were talking, and wondered if they dared creep closer for a look through the window. But when Nelson suggested it, Ted, after a moment's hesitation, turned him down.

"No, we can't take a chance on getting caught—at least not both of us. Besides, I think there's something more important to do. Mr. Gray couldn't have walked all the way out here. He must have hidden his car off the main road, the way we did. One of us ought to try to find it, and get the license number. Then if we don't get anything else out of this, we'll at least be able to find out who he is."

"I'll go," Nelson volunteered, "if you'll promise not to try anything while I'm gone."

"No, I won't," Ted promised. "I'll just stay here watching, and won't do a thing. You won't have to come to my rescue."

Nelson slipped away into the darkness. For ten or fifteen minutes nothing further happened, as far as Ted could determine. Then the light went out. A moment or two more, and the door opened. Mr. Gray stepped out, closed the door behind him, and started rapidly down the walk, finally disappearing in the shadows. Ted hoped he wouldn't meet Nelson, but didn't think it likely. Nelson was being too careful, and had had too much of a start.

But remembering that other person in the house, Ted could still not relax for a deep breath. He kept to his hiding place, his eyes fastened on the front door. And then, in a minute or so, the door opened again, and another man stepped out, equally as furtive as the first man. He, too, started down the walk, and as he stepped into the moonlit circle, Ted was nearly overcome with surprise and confusion.

It was Ken Kutler.

17.

Some Explanations

TED STEPPED boldly out into the moonlight.

"Hi, Ken," he called.

The reporter turned about slowly. Though momentarily startled, he was not too much surprised, for a newspaperman soon learns to assume that his rivals are close behind him. He shifted the brief case he was carrying from one hand to the other, and waited for Ted to come up to him.

"Well, Ken, how did you make out in your talk with Mr. Gray?"

"Mr. Gray? Is that his name? I didn't know that. But I wasn't talking with him, Ted. What do you think I am, anyway? I was hiding in a closet, trying to get a line on what was going on in this empty house."

"Then I take it you've got your story?"

"Oh, yes, Ted, I think I've got the thing pretty well figured out. Just a few loose threads yet, but they'll be tied up in the next couple of days. This is only Tuesday night, and I've got till Thursday noon for my story."

"I could get the story, too," Ted pointed out.

"You don't know the men involved—"

"I believe Nelson has Mr. Gray's license number, and I should be able to trace him from that. And if Mr. Denning is a telephone employee, I should be able to locate him, the same as you did."

"That's right, Ted, maybe you could." Ken hesitated for what seemed a long time. "Speaking as a reporter, Ted, I'd like to have the story all for myself; again, speaking as a reporter, I realize you're entitled to the story, if you can get it. Now may I speak as a friend?"

"I sure wish you would, Ken."

"Then my advice is: don't touch this story. You're in a peculiar spot, Ted, and there are some pitfalls in the use of this story that you aren't aware of. The difference between you and me right now is that I have my editor back of me, and you don't. Mr. Dobson is in the hospital, and you couldn't possibly use this story without his approval. Even if I were to give you an exact copy of my own story, Mr. Dobson wouldn't use it until he could check on a number of things."

Ted considered. He knew that Ken, though a hard-hitting reporter, was always frank and sincere. Ken, speaking as a friend and not as a reporter, had asked him not to touch the story, and Ted knew Ken must have some very definite reasons for his advice.

"All right, Ken, that's good enough for me. I won't touch it for now. Anyway, I guess one big story in a week is enough for me. And you can have that license number, if you want it."

"Thanks, Ted." Ken seemed pleased. "Then suppose we pick up Nelson, and go over to my place, where we can try to get this whole thing ironed out. Not quite everything, Ted—I'm going to hold out a few things on you, because I think some of these big-city reporters will be calling you in the next day or two, just the way they did today, and it will be better for both of us if you don't know all the answers."

After a very much surprised Nelson had been added to

their party, they drove over to Ken's, where they gathered around the kitchen table and drank hot chocolate. Ken took up his story.

"I'll tell you how I've got this operation figured out. It was Mr. Denning, of course, who was back of it. He has another name at the telephone company, and he took out the option on the house under still a different name, and perhaps he's been using half-a-dozen other names. Perhaps we never will know which is his own.

"It was Ted's tip suggesting a telephone employee which first put me on the right track. At the beginning I was very skeptical, and I had good reason for it. Up until then my thinking had centered on the likelihood that it was an inside job. It was obvious that the thief would have to know a good deal about what was going on in the Highway Department, when the plans were finished, where Mr. Montague was likely to keep them, and so on. Still, I thought, Ted was impressed by all these telephone shenanigans, and he might have a point.

"It occurred to me that there might be two of them in it together, a Highway Department employee and a telephone employee. If there were, it might be difficult to prove the necessary link between them. But then I reasoned, a man would much prefer to handle it by himself, if he could. This would lessen the risk of a slip up and discovery. So then I began to look for a *former* Highway Department employee who was a new telephone employee, and in this way I easily located Mr. Denning. He was in a position to handle his maneuvers by telephone, and he still had a pretty good idea what was going on in the Highway Department. Perhaps he had friends in the department who quite innocently supplied him with all the information he needed.

"Where we were led astray was in believing that the thief would speculate in land, most likely at Milford, but possibly somewhere else along the highway route. I think this is the lead Mr. Montague was following up, and if my experience is any test, it will get him nowhere. Mr. Denning was either too smart or too broke to do that. He realized that this was a way he might get caught, and besides, he probably didn't have the money to buy up options.

"No, Mr. Denning's plan of operations was much different. He intended to sell these plans to other persons, who could then buy up options or do anything else they pleased with the information. But there was one big danger he wished to, avoid. He wanted to destroy any possibility of a link being established between himself and the persons who bought the plans. He would be dealing with some rather shady characters, and he didn't want them to be in a position to blackmail him, or to turn state's evidence against him. Also, if they should be caught and picked up and questioned, the police would have no way of tracing a connection back to him.

"To accomplish all this he needed a telephone number at which his customers could call and ask him questions. Perhaps one customer would refer other customers to him, and he couldn't always call them. Besides, some of these persons calling were probably completely upright persons, and he didn't want to arouse their suspicions until he could feel them out. Yes, he needed an ordinary telephone, but one which couldn't be traced afterward. He also needed a house for the telephone, a house that couldn't be traced back to him, a house where his customers could come to look over the plans and leave their payments. The whole essence of his scheme was that he would never meet his customers face to face!

"Mr. Denning was lucky enough to find an empty house that answered his purpose, probably through the telephone records, and rigged up the telephone. Then, by posing as a telephone repairman, he got into Mr. Montague's apartment and stole the plans from the steel cabinet."

"That's something I don't understand," Ted interrupted. "Why should he take the plans? Wouldn't simply looking at them have been enough? He could have found out whether the Milford interchange was going to be built without ever taking the plans. Then they'd never have been missed, and he couldn't have been caught."

"Well, Ted, that might be true if he were planning on speculating himself. But remember, he wanted to sell these plans to other people, and they would have to see the real plans before they were willing to put down their money. I do think this, though, that Mr. Denning thought he had a month to work, and intended to return the plans before the month was up, so that no one would know they were gone.

"Not everything Mr. Denning did was perfectly logical, as we are able to see now. But criminals may become flustered, especially when something goes wrong with the original plan. Mr. Denning had to play it by ear, so to speak, and he may have made some mistakes.

"The theft occurred on Monday morning. After getting the plans, Mr. Denning left by train for Forestdale, and here is where the first important thing went wrong. We've wondered how he managed to lose the plans. You'd think he would try to be very careful with them, since they were so valuable to him. But for the very reason that these plans were valuable, they were also dangerous to him. He *thought* he had thirty days of grace, but he couldn't be sure about it, and his conscience was busy. If you've ever done something wrong, and then imagined that everyone was looking at you and every innocent remark was directed against you, you can perhaps appreciate how he felt.

"Under these circumstances I think it very likely that Mr. Denning simply put the notebook up on the rack in the train, and spent most of the journey forward in the smoking car. The less time he actually had the plans in his possession, the less likelihood of his getting caught. But then as the train pulled into Forestdale something went wrong—and unless Mr. Denning finally tells us, and I doubt that he's the talkative sort, we may never know exactly what it was. I can picture it in one of two different ways. The first is that Mrs. Conway awoke suddenly on the train, confused and flustered, and accidentally thrust the notebook into her own shopping bag.

"But I also see it another way. Remember there was a lot of confusion at the station due to this reception for the Olympics star. Mr. Denning looked out and saw the police, and thought they were waiting for *him*, and became panicky. He thrust the plans into Mrs. Conway's bag himself. He may have thought she was getting off at Forestdale, and that if she managed to get past the police all right, he could overtake her, explain the mistake, and recover the plans. However, Mrs. Conway did not get off at Forestdale. Probably Mr. Denning was obliged to get off ahead of her, and thought she would presently follow. Then, to his amazement, she never got off at all, and he stood there and watched the train chug off, carrying the plans he had gone to so much trouble to get!

"We can't tell exactly what went on in his mind. He realized that Mrs. Conway probably would have no idea what was in the package, and that she would be only too glad to return it. Therefore, the best thing Mr. Denning could think of was to put an ad in the Forestdale *Town Crier*. He may have tried other methods of locating Mrs. Conway, too, but we don't know about them. Anyway, he phoned in the ad, believing this would be preferable to a personal appearance, alert to see whether Ted had heard about the missing notebook and was suspicious about it. In this ad he had to be careful about describing the lost article. He wanted to describe it sufficiently so that Mrs. Conway would recognize it, but not sufficiently so that Mr. Montague or anyone else would recognize it as the highway plans. Here again something went wrong, for Ted printed a more inclusive description of the notebook than Mr. Denning desired, and Mr. Montague did recognize it. Because of his unexpected return, he had already discovered the loss of the plans.

"Anyway, the ad was placed, and Mr. Denning realized that he would have to give Ted some sort of identification— if not an address, at least a telephone number. Since he already had a telephone available, he gave the number Forestdale 8106. On thinking it over, though, he felt he would have to appear at the *Town Crier* office at least once in order to establish good faith and keep Ted's suspicions from being aroused. He did so, coming early before any answer could reasonably be expected because he also wanted to get there before any storm had had a chance to brew. He arranged to have the missing article sent out to him, and ordinarily this might have worked out very well for him.

"Owing to the popularity of my rival paper, the *Town Crier*, the ad was seen and the article promptly returned by Mrs. Conway. Now once more something went wrong, for Ted decided to return the article in person, and so discovered the empty house. From the exact timing of that telephone call in the empty house I believe that Mr. Denning was able to *see* you boys at the empty house, and so he must have been in the gardener's cottage at the time. He waited anxiously, hoping you might leave the package inside the door when you failed to get an answer. Instead, he saw you walking away from the house and back toward the car, still carrying the package. He had to do something fast, or else he'd never get the plans back without making a lot of explanations he didn't care to make.

"He rang the telephone, and Ted answered. Mr. Denning was able to convince Ted it would be all right to leave the plans in the empty house, and Ted did. All well and good. Mr. Denning had recovered the missing plans, and that was the most important thing for him. However, things still weren't as satisfactory as he'd like them. If Ted should ever come out to the empty house again, and find it still empty, his suspicions would be aroused. Besides, there was the chance he might grow inquisitive about that telephone number. The telephone call to Mr. White was made in the hope of lulling Ted's suspicions. Nevertheless, there was nothing for it but to change his base of operations to some other empty house."

"I still don't understand how he worked those telephone calls," Nelson maintained.

"I called him at Forestdale 8106, and he answered," Ted put in, "and later I took a call on a telephone marked with the same number."

"And there weren't any wires," Nelson added.

"Well, let's see," Ken resumed. "You phoned from the newspaper office, dialed Forestdale 8106, and got Mr. Denning. But you don't know where Mr. Denning was at the time. You thought he was at the empty house, but I doubt it. I've already said I thought he could see you when you visited the empty house, and that he was staying at the cottage. And that, I think, is where the telephone was.

"Mr. Denning had managed at the telephone company to get Forestdale 8106 hooked up with the cottage. I don't think he could have done something like this in a large telephone office—it would have to go through too many departments and require the help of other people. But in a small company, and under a dial system, I believe it is possible to plug a line in on a number that is supposed to be discontinued. Of course you'd have to know a great deal about the company setup, its system of billing, how the lines are checked, and so on. And you wouldn't want to receive any long-distance calls on such a telephone, because records are kept of such calls.

"There was always a possibility of accidental discovery, but criminals are obliged to take chances. Perhaps if it were discovered, he could pretend it was only an honest mistake, or perhaps he had the evidence so covered up that even if it was discovered it would not point to him as the culprit. When Ted dialed Forestdale 8106 the next day, and got the operator who said there wasn't any such number, that was the truth. The number had been disconnected by Mr. Denning by that time."

"But there wasn't any wire," Nelson insisted.

"Yes, Nelson, there was a wire. You remember you didn't go around to the back of the house the first time you were out there, and by the second time you were there the cable had been removed. But there was a cable, leading from the cottage to a pole around a bend in the road. It didn't go out to the front at all."

"What about the call I took in the empty house?" asked Ted.

"That was on a direct line leading back to the cottage, Ted, where Mr. Denning had an extra telephone. He rang the bell in the empty house, and talked to you directly. Of course you didn't know where he was at the time. I believe he had arranged the setup deliberately, since he didn't want his customers to know where he was calling from, but wanted to be close to the scene. Of course the cable between the cottage and the house was also taken down before you came back the second time."

"Then after he moved his operation out of the empty house," Ted went on, "did he go on to Everett House?"

"No, not Everett House. That was too far away from

things, and it was outside the area of the Forestdale telephone service."

"Then why did Mr. Denning lure us out there?"

"I think it possible he had several different motives, Ted. Maybe he really hoped to scare you off the case, thinking you might be closing in on him. Maybe he was trying to pump you for information, hoping to find out what the police were doing, or whether there was any plan for releasing the road plans to the newspapers, which would have put an end to his operation. This doesn't quite convince me. I think there was another reason, but it's one of the things I'm going to hold out on you for the time being."

"I suppose it's old-fashioned to think telephones need wires," Nelson came in, "but how did he talk over the telephone at Everett House with not a telephone pole in sight?"

"Well, he had this old-fashioned telephone rigged up in the house, and the wires led under the floor and to the outside wall. At this outside wall a connection could quickly be made with a cable leading off into the woods. He would have to stand some distance off when talking to you, so you wouldn't hear his natural voice, and perhaps also he wanted a place of concealment, even though it was dark. There was another telephone at the end of the cable, and a battery powered the contraption. As soon as the call was completed, it was the work of a moment to disconnect or to yank off the connection, and drag the cable off into the woods, so that no trace remained by the time you got outside."

"Then he must have switched his operation to the house on Liggett Road by this time," Ted observed. "How did he work the telephone there? We know there weren't any wires when that telephone was ringing, and there wasn't anybody around outside."

Ken laughed. "I think Nelson called the turn on that one, Ted. You're just old-fashioned. There was a wire, and the telephone was connected up, but the cable was *underground*. This is a fairly common practice in congested districts, though it is rare out here in the country. But it is technically feasible, especially in a new development where all the utilities can be buried at once, where the distances are not too great, and where it is unnecessary to worry too much about costs."

"So there goes a good ghost story down the drain," Nelson lamented. "But I'm still not sure I get this. Exactly how did he deal with his customers?"

"I imagine he had prospects, people he thought might be interested, and sounded them out by telephone. Or perhaps some prospects called him, on the days when he was out at the empty house. After the preliminary negotiations, he would give them the address of the house. They would come out at a time when he wasn't there. They'd come in and look the plans over. There was a telephone, and I suppose if they had any further questions they could reach him at a public booth where he was standing by—I noticed a number written by the phone, and I'm sure it will be untraceable. The customer looked the plans over, decided they were authentic, got the particular piece of information he wanted, deposited his money there, and left."

"Left?" Nelson ejaculated. "Why not take the plans with him?"

"Because Mr. Denning had a big advantage over his customers. He knew who they were, but they didn't know who he was. If they took the plans, he could make an anonymous call to the police, the person might be questioned, and he certainly wouldn't want to be found with the plans in his possession."

"But would he have to leave the money?" asked Ted. "Now that he had the information, he could simply walk out."

"Perhaps, Ted, but still not likely. They still didn't know

who they were dealing with, how much power he held, or what he might do to them. No, it was easier to pay up and not take chances."

"Then there were a lot of other people involved, weren't there," Ted mused, "a lot of other people who may never be caught."

"There were other people involved, Ted, undoubtedly. We already know about Mr. Gray, who was one of Mr. Denning's customers, but we can't tell how many other customers Mr. Denning had, nor can we tell how deeply they were involved. Some of them may have regarded the undertaking as perfectly legitimate—they were simply being let in on the ground floor of a good thing. Possibly Mr. Denning represented the plans as coming through a leak in a private engineering firm, and not actually being stolen. Some people may have seen the deal as shady, but still legal. Others may have known all along they were skirting the law, but were willing to take a chance. Of course, by the time they actually saw the plans, knew they were stolen from the Highway Department, and put down their money, they realized they were breaking the law, but they may have felt it was too late to back out by that time."

"So that's how it all happened," said Nelson, shaking his head in wonder. "Somehow I didn't think all of this was ever going to be explained."

"It must have kept you hopping," Ted observed, "getting all this."

"Yes, it did. Of course some of it is still surmise, but I'm pretty sure of my basic facts. It was a clever enough scheme —rather elaborate, whereas the simplest plan is often the best—but Mr. Denning has the kind of mind that prefers the intricate scheme. Unfortunately for him, at least three things went wrong: he lost the plans, Mr. Montague discovered the theft sooner than expected, and Ted returned the plans in person to the empty house. That was his gamble, and it didn't quite pay off. They tell us crime doesn't pay, and though I can't prove it from my own experience, I'm willing to take their word for it as of now."

18.

The Angry Man

THE NEXT MORNING Ted had several more calls from the daily newspapers. He wasn't sure what to tell them. He was willing to give them anything he could that would help them verify the story he had published the previous day. But he didn't feel he could break his promise to Mr. Montague and mention the missing plans, and he didn't want to say anything that might spoil Ken's story.

Ken had done considerable leg work to locate the criminal and figure out his method of operation, and was certainly deserving of a scoop. But the story had broken on the wrong day, as far as Ken was concerned. On their papers the best time for a story to break was eleven o'clock in the morning, on Monday or Thursday. Reporters on daily papers had fewer worries about the moment when stories broke. A reporter on a weekly or a semi-weekly paper, however, often has to cover up his story for a time, fearful lest a daily reporter jump in and get it into print ahead of him.

Because Ted was trying to help out Ken, some of the answers he gave were very evasive. He felt satisfied that the reporters hadn't gotten very much out of him. They knew he was covering up something but couldn't find out what it was. In return, he had to undergo some good-natured kidding about small-town newspapers. He also learned from the reporters of pressure being put on the governor to release the whole story about the road plans. Ted's name was being mentioned in the stories the dailies were printing. He was something of a state-wide celebrity, even though the people in Forestdale hadn't caught on to it yet.

Nelson dropped into the office to discuss the case. He was most puzzled because so far no arrest had been announced. Once an arrest was made, the radio stations and the daily papers would probably have the story, even if it was too early for the *Town Crier* or the *News-Record*.

"Deadline trouble," Ted decided. "Ken would like to put off the arrest until it hits his deadline, if he can. He's cooperated with the police in the past, so I suppose they'd try to help him out if they could."

"Isn't that taking a chance Denning might get away?"

"I imagine Ken's got that angle covered pretty well."

Another point was that so far Ted was the only person who had seen Mr. Denning. The thief had even managed to hide from his own customers.

"But he felt he had to come into the office just once," Nelson recalled, "so you wouldn't be suspicious about him and would mail the plans. Do you think you could identify him again?"

"I think Ken's got this case so well sewed up that the matter of an identification won't come up. But I imagine Mr. Denning must have been partly disguised when he came to the office. He wouldn't want to make it too easy for me to recognize him again."

"That mustache!" Nelson exclaimed. "You mentioned that before. It could have been a false one, and he took it off after he left."

"Sure." Ted grinned. "And it could have been a *real* one. Maybe he shaved it off after he left here, and that was the reason he had to make sure I didn't see him again without the mustache."

"But we still haven't gotten the highway plans back. That won't interfere with the construction of the highway, will it?"

"Oh, no, there must be duplicate sets available. The important thing is what the thief may have been able to do with them. I'd feel better about it if we had them back."

"Anyway, I guess Ken's done a pretty good job on this story. I wonder why he doesn't go for a career on a big city paper, the way Ron did?"

"I guess he could have it if he wanted it," Ted remarked. "But he told me once a reporter like that just wouldn't be *him*. He likes a small paper where he can be more independent. He'll be editor there someday—maybe owner, too."

Another thing on Ted's mind was his relation with Carl Allison. Carl, of course, had been pleased that the *Town Crier* had gotten the story about Mr. Lamont, although a little put out that the story had been Ted's instead of his own. In his opinion he was the reporter and Ted was the office help. But Ted's explanation that he had happened to stumble upon Mr. Lamont while visiting Nelson's aunt had satisfied him.

Ken's story, however, was a different matter, and Ted was expecting fireworks to explode. Still, what else could he have done? Ted had passed on to Ken his hunch that a telephone man might be guilty, but later he had mentioned the same thing to Carl, and Carl hadn't thought it worth following up —although to do him credit he had been very busy. As for going out after hours and watching an empty house night after night until something happened, Carl would never have done that. It wasn't his idea of how a newspaper reporter should work. He wanted efficiency, and the efficient thing was to rely on the police and not waste your own time. Well,

Miss Monroe would be back at the end of the week, and with her in charge once more, Ted and Carl would have very little to quarrel about.

Shortly after Nelson left, another telephone call came through.

"Ted Wilford?" It was Mr. Montague's voice. He was clearly much annoyed.

"This is Ted Wilford speaking."

"Well, Ted, this is the very first moment I've had a chance to call you since your story on Mr. Lamont was brought to my attention. I don't have to tell you what a hornets' nest you've stirred up. I feel you've broken your promise to me. If you had any knowledge that a public official was acting improperly, you could have come quietly to me, and I would have looked into it. But no, you people always have to watch out for your little stories."

But if it had been such a "little" story, Mr. Montague wouldn't have been so upset. Ted's jaw was set and stubborn, but he said nothing. He felt he hadn't broken his promise, that he had acted as a newspaperman ought to, as Ken had advised him to act. But there was little use in trying to explain this to Mr. Montague. The state auditor appeared to hold the view that the purpose of a newspaper was to serve the government, not the people.

"With all this publicity I don't suppose we'll ever get the plans back now," Mr. Montague went on. "Well, the governor's called a press conference for Friday morning. I want you to come to my apartment tonight and help me work out what sort of story we're going to give to the press." He didn't give Ted a chance to refuse, but said a curt "Good-by" and hung up.

Ted felt his cheeks burning. He wondered what Ken would have done in a situation like this, and it occurred to him that the easiest way to find out would be to ask him. After all, if the auditor was annoyed now, he was going to be really annoyed when Ken's story came out.

He was able to reach Ken promptly, and explained his conversation with Mr. Montague.

"Why do you suppose he really wants to see me, Ken? I can't decide for him what sort of statement he ought to make to the papers. Do you suppose he just wants to chew me out some more?"

"That's probably part of it, Ted. But I imagine he's mostly interested in finding out how much you know, and how much the *Town Crier* is going to print."

"Then you think I ought to go?"

"Yes, Ted, I do. Oh, not just because Mr. Montague is an important person and asked you to come. But when you've got a legitimate grievance, it's often better to make it known rather than to sit home pouting about it. What would you say if I were to come along? If Mr. Montague thinks he can browbeat a young reporter, maybe I can straighten him out with a few facts."

"I'd like it, Ken, only I don't want to seem to be hiding behind you."

"Don't worry about that, Ted. I'm in this just as deeply as you are."

Mr. Montague was surprised to see Ken Kutler, whom he knew slightly, but he didn't allow that to deter him. He was alone in the apartment when they came. He opened the door himself, closed it after them, and almost without a greeting began to state his opinion of the affair in no uncertain terms.

"I suppose we've got to expect something like this from a small country paper that suffers from delusions of grandeur. I'm not saying so much about your returning the plans to the thief, Ted, for I know you're young and inexperienced. But I did think, when you promised not to print anything about the plans being stolen, I could rely on it for a while."

"I don't think I broke my promise," Ted maintained. "I promised not to print anything about the theft. My story didn't say anything about the missing plans."

"No, but in your story about Mr. Lamont there was an implication of a leak with the highway plans, and the daily papers were quick to jump on it. I can't begin to tell you all the trouble you've caused. This reflects upon our entire state administration. The governor may decide he'll have to release the plans to the public, and he doesn't want to do that just yet. The budget isn't ready, and he can't be sure of the concurrence of the Legislature. Maybe there'll have to be a special session, and right now in this summer heat that would be bad politically. And all this mess came about for the sake of a two-bit story in your scandal sheet!"

Ted could tell that Ken's temper was rising just as rapidly as his own, but he spoke calmly:

"Mr. Montague, we're newspapermen. Our newspapers pay our salaries, and in the end the public decides whether or not it likes our work. If anything we write happens to embarrass a public official, that's too bad, but it's part of our job. When newspapers begin to cover up for official mistakes, then our country will really be in a sorry way. I don't feel that Ted broke any promise to you; as a matter of fact, he acted upon my advice in using the story. He promised not to interfere with the recovery of the plans, but he didn't promise to sit on this story, and any possible related story, from now until the end of time. As for myself, I feel that I am released from any promises I made to you once the plans are recovered. Isn't that correct?"

"I suppose so, but—"

Ken reached down for the brief case he had brought along with him, the same brief case he had been carrying the night he visited the empty house on Liggett Road.

"Well, then, here you are!"

From his case he extracted a red-leather notebook and

handed it to the auditor. Ted's eyes nearly popped. Then this was one of the things Ken had been holding out on him.

The auditor looked startled. He took a key from his pocket, hastily opened the notebook, and examined the plans.

"Yes, these are the plans, all right. How did you get them?"

Quickly Ken explained about the affair of the empty house, how Mr. Denning had left the notebook—for which he must have furnished himself and his clients with duplicate keys—to be examined by his customers. Ken had searched the house but had been unable to find where the notebook was hidden, until Mr. Gray arrived and took it from its place of conceal-ment, a secret compartment beneath a drawer. Then after Mr. Gray had left, Ken had calmly appropriated the note-book from its hiding place and walked off with it.

"Has there been an arrest?"

"Not yet."

"Why not?" asked Mr. Montague sharply.

"Because the police thought it would help their case if they could make the arrest immediately after Mr. Denning re-turned to pick up the money in the secret compartment. This would definitely link him to the scene. Of course they are watching him, and if he should attempt to leave town he would be picked up."

"Wouldn't he have gone out to the empty house to pick up the money immediately after Mr. Gray left?"

"He couldn't. He works a changing shift, and I checked his working schedule."

"And what charge is going to be placed?"

The auditor seemed unduly excited, but Ken was calm. "Under the laws of our state, a suspect may be held for twenty-four hours without a charge being placed. The police will hold off as long as they can, because they understand about my deadline troubles. I've worked hard on this story, and there's no sense letting a big daily cut in on me."

"What about Mr. Gray? Will he be arrested, too?"

"I don't know. That's up to the police."

Mr. Montague still looked very dissatisfied as he fingered the notebook.

"Of course I'm glad to get the plans back, and glad the thief is caught. But the thief may have had photostats made —of course he did—and we don't know how many other persons have seen these plans—"

"No, and probably we never will know. I suppose you'd like me to kill this story, then?"

"If you would—"

"No dice. The plans are back, and my story comes out Friday morning. But let me tell you a little something—I still don't think I have the complete story. Suppose I tell you how I have things figured out. You haven't been especially worried that some unscrupulous persons might profit from the theft. You've been worried about how this theft was going to reflect upon you. And I must say it doesn't put you in a very good light. You took these plans home with you, put them in a steel cabinet which anyone could easily force open, and then left for a month's vacation! That was almost an invitation to a prospective thief to come in and help himself.

"This was what started me thinking. I thought, now what goes with this Mr. Montague? He's done something that appears either very careless or very stupid. Yet I know he's not a stupid man, and I know he never became state auditor by doing such careless things as this. It may be that things aren't at all as they appear.

"Then there was that scene you staged in the *Town Crier* office, and the one you are apparently staging right now, assuming great anger and indignation. Occasionally a public official will show anger at an unexpected charge, but generally speaking he knows his best bet, his best angle on public relations, is to appear calm and smooth in public. And especially there's no use arguing with newspapermen, who have the last word in print anyhow. So I began to wonder, is Mr. Montague really as angry as he appears, or is this just an act he's putting on for some reason or other?

"Then I came up with what I thought was the answer. Mr. Montague wasn't stupid, and he wasn't careless, and he wasn't angry. The only alternate solution, then, was that the highway plans were never in that notebook, were never in that steel cabinet, were never stolen!"

Mr. Montague blustered, "Now wait a minute. Do you think I'm lying about all this? Do you think I'm in league with the thief?"

"No, Mr. Montague," said Ken smoothly, "I don't think that at all. I merely think that there were *two* sets of highway plans. Of course on any project as huge as this thruway business there are a lot of differences of opinion, but most of these could be handled within the Highway Department itself. The biggest difference concerned the Milford interchange, and this was something so big that it had to be handled on the top level. I think the Highway Department prepared alternate sets of plans, one showing the Milford interchange and one without the Milford interchange. *Both* plans were sent on to the governor's office for a decision.

"My opinion is that a decision was reached some weeks ago, when the governor decided to recommend *against* the Milford interchange. The decision was communicated to you, so that you could incorporate it into your forthcoming budget message. The real highway plans, the accepted highway plans, went into your office safe, and the discarded plans were taken home and carelessly placed in your steel cabinet."

"Then you mean those plans we were searching for were of no value at all?" asked Ted blankly.

"Oh, yes, Ted, they were very valuable, although Mr. Montague didn't realize it till afterward. They were valuable in a purely negative way. Look at it this way: if the thief knew that these were not the real plans, and that these plans showed the Milford exchange, then by inference the real plans would *not* show the Milford exchange. If the thief knew this for sure, he might have turned his knowledge into almost as much profit as he hoped to make by stealing the real plans."

"This is all supposition so far," said Mr. Montague stiffly.

"But a reasonable supposition, I believe. If the real plans had been stolen, you would have been faced with a dilemma. You'd like to cover up the theft in order to trap the thief more easily, but you also would have a duty to the public. I feel sure your decision would have been to release the plans immediately. But if they were the false plans, then you knew you didn't have to worry about the public. The only persons who would be hurt were those people who purchased the plans illegally and bought up worthless options. In many cases these were people whom the law would not be able to reach, and so you were quite willing that they should squander their money foolishly. By pretending these were the real plans, the thief would not be alerted. At the same time, if the papers should get on to the story, you were in a position to deny officially that the plans had ever been stolen. But you were hoping that wouldn't happen for a while. Let the thief keep operating until, perhaps, he would overstep the line, and so might get caught."

Mr. Montague seemed to be debating with himself. Finally his decision was reached and he became much more affable, as all his anger disappeared.

"I'm afraid I owe you an apology, Mr. Kutler. Your analysis is correct. The governor will release the real plans at his conference on Friday morning, and until then I was willing to let these people the law can't touch continue to invest their money in worthless options. I didn't mean everything I said about country papers, and I must say that I mean it even less right now. I hope you don't mind my tongue-lashing. You've proved to me that high-quality men can be found even on small papers."

"Oh, I didn't mind," said Ken good-naturedly, "as long as you didn't think you were putting anything over on me. There's one way you could still hurt me—by calling in the daily papers tomorrow and explaining the whole thing."

"I'm not likely to do that," said the auditor genially. "We scheduled the conference for Friday morning, and I'll let it stand. I'm not interested in talking to the newspapers any more than I have to. They've given me a rough time lately, and I'm satisfied to let them stew awhile. Anyway, you did catch the thief and explain his operation, so I think you're perfectly entitled to your news beat."

He extended his hand, and shook each of theirs warmly. "I always like to have newspapermen on my side when I can. I hope that we'll meet again, Mr. Kutler, and if it's in the course of business, that I'll have you on my side. You're too tough an opponent for me. Ted, don't feel too bad about your mistake. I could tell you about some bloopers I've pulled in my time, but I'm saving them until I'm retired and write my autobiography."

Outside, Ken said, "Well, I guess that's the end of it. He isn't such a bad sort after all, is he? Oh, about your adventure at Everett House, Ted. I said I thought Mr. Denning had another reason for getting you up there. I think, although he appeared to be threatening you, he was actually pumping you for information. I suspect he may have had some doubts in his own mind about whether those were the real plans, and he wanted to see if you knew anything about it."

"Did it matter to him whether they were the real plans, as long as he was going to sell them anyhow?"

"Perhaps it did. He may have intended to buy some options himself, or he may have been afraid of what his customers would do if the plans were false. But it may be that he simply had his own peculiar standards of honesty toward his customers. I've known some queer characters like that."

He started the car and they drove slowly toward home. "Just one more thing, Ted," said Ken as they neared Forestdale. "It looks like I am still going to have my big story. I know you've promised me not to touch it, and that's one reason I've been so open with you. But don't think I don't know what you've done. You beat me out on the Mr. Lamont angle. You gave me the tip on the telephone man. When I located the empty house, there you were sitting out in the bushes, breathing hot down my collar. If we ever tangle on another news story, I'm not going to concede you one little inch. I can't afford to."

"Thanks, Ken," said Ted, getting out of the car in front of his home. He felt pleased that Ken regarded him as a full-fledged rival. "That's just the way I want it."

19.

Printer's Ink

WITH THE appearance of Ken's story and the release of the highway plans by the governor the mystery came to an end. And with Miss Monroe back, looking almost as well as ever, Ted's responsibility for the paper was over.

But now, with the story virtually ended, Ted felt it was time to print the tale of how he had turned the supposed highway plans over to the thief. It was the one sour note in an otherwise bright picture. The *Town Crier* would come out on Tuesday, which was the same day as the senior picnic, and Ted knew he would let himself in for some kidding. Coming from his friends, that might not be so easy to take.

Mr. Dobson continued to show improvement, so that Ted was able to see him at last. As he entered the hospital room, the editor motioned him over to the bed, and shook his hand.

"It seems to me I've a good deal to thank you for, Ted."

"No, you haven't, not for anything at all," Ted objected. "I haven't even begun to pay you back for everything you've done for Ronald and me. I'm only glad I could help a little, and wish I could have done it better."

"You've done a splendid job, Ted. Very few young men could have stepped into the breach the way you did. I don't know all the details, but I've been able to judge the results.

I notice that Ken Kutler gave you considerable credit in his scoop."

"I know." Ted grinned. "I may have some trouble living that down—a write-up in a rival paper. I'm not sure I shouldn't have tried to get the story for our own paper, but Ken warned me against it."

"And quite rightly, Ted. There were some serious pitfalls you might have fallen into. For instance, if you'd claimed the highway plans were stolen, and it turned out these weren't the real plans, it would have been very embarrassing for you. And Mr. Denning, as it now appears, was admitted into Mr. Montague's apartment by the building superintendent, which isn't the same thing as burglary. Then it makes a difference whether something of value was taken, and in this case the thing stolen was worthless. The wire taps were so well covered up they might have been difficult to prove. And you'll notice how careful Ken was not to accuse Mr. Gray of any crime, since it now seems to be a fact that he had nothing at all to do with the actual theft."

"There are laws against receiving stolen property. Isn't receiving stolen information the same thing?"

"Possibly, though harder to prove. Mr. Gray and the other customers could pretend to various degrees of innocence on the kind of operation it was. Anyway, it's up to the police, not the newspapers, to decide what charges ought to be pressed. It was best that you stayed out of it."

"But I've made some mistakes—"

"Just as anybody would stepping into a job that was new and important and complicated."

"But now that the case is over, don't you think we ought to print a story about how I turned the notebook over to the thief?"

Mr. Dobson's eyes twinkled. "Oh, yes, Ted, I'm sure we ought to print it. The trouble is, Ken's story has made old

news out of all this. But I think there's a story we can use—
a feature story, written in the first person, telling about your
whole participation in the case, including the part you
played in helping to solve it."

"A first-person story? But that means—" Ted stopped in
wonder.

"Yes, Ted, that means you're going to get your first professional by-line. No, don't thank me," he went on as Ted
tried to interrupt. "You're a little young for it, but I think
you fully deserve it."

Ted felt a warm glow of pleasure. This was appreciation
expressed in the way a young reporter likes best. But Mr.
Dobson refused his thanks, and all Ted could do was to
change the subject to cover up his own embarrassment.

"How are you feeling, Mr. Dobson?"

"Oh, it's no fun lying here flat on your back, and I won't
pretend it is. But the cast is coming off next week, and after
the X rays maybe the doctor will let me get back on my feet.
I won't mind crutches, as long as I can get down to the office.
Tell me, Ted, are you planning to stay on at the *Town Crier*
for a while?"

"I don't know. I don't feel as though I'm needed now."

"There'll always be a place for you there, Ted, if you want
it. But at the same time I don't want you to give up any more
of your summer plans just to help me out."

"I don't really have any plans just now, but I guess I'll hang
around for a while until I'm sure Miss Monroe is caught up."

"You and Carl getting along all right?"

"Well," said Ted carefully, not wanting to tell him about
the quarrel he had had with Carl over Ken's story, for he felt
he had defended his own part successfully, "I guess we
understand each other a lot better now."

It was time to go, and Mr. Dobson smiled as he held out
his hand once more. "This newspaper fever gets in your

blood, doesn't it? I caught it when I was even younger than you are, and I never got over it. I don't think you will, either."

Ted felt unusually happy as he left the hospital. He was all set to enjoy the senior picnic, and let them kid him if they wanted to. With his own by-lined story they couldn't say anything to hurt him now.

One thing, though—at the previous year's picnic he had skinned his elbow playing baseball, and it had bled a little. He hoped the same thing wouldn't happen again. He wasn't ready yet to let his friends know he had printer's ink instead of blood running through his veins.

Printed in Great Britain
by Amazon